HIDDEN TRUTH

HIDDEN TRUTH

Naomi Skye

Contents

1

Trepidation

After close to fifty years caged and chained inside the disgustingly dark, cramped, and lifeless Halls of Trepidation, Yarra White was well aware that she was to be accompanied everywhere she went in shackles and at least five heavily armed guards. Of the thousands of people who resided within the halls, not one by choice, most were escorted everywhere they went like the prisoners they were. Yarra was the only one they paid special attention to.

Yarra was the one they beat when the elderly or the children collapsed and could no longer work. Yarra was the one they used whenever fresh slaves were brought in and a pretty young thing caught the eye of one of the guards. They had their way with the terrified girl right in front of her as she screamed and Yarra bellowed curses to the heavens – then they moved onto her.

Why? Because in all the forty-seven years Yarra had been locked and chained alone in the underground prison, she had not broken, had not showed fear or regret or remorse – except for that one time, but no one spoke of that time. The guards had discovered early on that this was the only way to hurt her, to make her watch as they hurt others.

But she didn't hold it against them. That was to be expected of Verstra's most volatile and unpredictable assassin. They made sure she was constantly chained. Where some prisoners were only cuffed after their magic went out of control or when they had refused to follow instructions, Yarra's shackles were her constant companion. But that too was to be expected. What she did not expect, however, was the hooded man at her side, as there was now.

His vice-like grip on her arm led her up and up through the winding labyrinth of tunnels and halls and then past rows and rows of rooms that housed the many guards and overseers of Trepidation until she was hopelessly, unimaginably lost.

Except she wasn't. Instead, she was just insulted, insulted that they thought they could confuse her like this. With all the twisting and turning, they had sought to confuse her, but she had not failed to notice when they passed the same room not once or twice but five times. All they had done was familiarise her with the upper levels of the halls. *Idiots.*

Had she wanted to escape, all she would have to do was turn right and then take the second left and follow a final right to freedom.

She was insulted that they had forgotten who she was, that they thought five guards were enough to contain her should she choose to make a break for it. Even cuffed, with her magic stifled, she was a force to be reckoned with. It was an insult, plain and simple, to see that they had forgotten that.

They entered a particularly long hallway, as dark and as damp as the rest of the prison, their footsteps making soft wet thwacks on the ground. She looked at the man at her side, could see nothing of his face or features. He was a mystery to her, another tactic to intimidate her into submission. She peered up at him as if she could push away the dark shadows with will alone and gave him a small smile, crinkling eyes that hadn't lost their brightness despite the years she'd spent underground.

The man did not smile back.

Yarra supposed she should be flattered despite the multiple insults heaped upon her. He was so clearly going to an unbelievable amount of effort to intimidate her. She had thought herself well acquainted with all the powerful houses across Verstra, yet when he'd introduced himself, Kayneth Kor, she had had no clue who he was, only vague memories, aged memories hundreds of years past – and a nagging sense that things had changed in the outside world.

'Where are we going? To the beginning? To the light?' she asked sweetly, batting filthy matted lashes at him. 'You know, this would be a whole lot easier if you just told me where we were going and what House Violet has to do with it.'

Oh, she was not so lost in the despairs of Trepidation that she had missed the ring pressed deep into the flesh or her arm or its purple colouring. All those in service to the Rainbow wore a ring such as that; the ring's specific colour indicated loyalty to a specific house.

'The long game is a good one,' she said, 'but eventually, all souls belong to me. Might as well spill now.'

In another lifetime, she had been pretty, not drop-dead gorgeous but pretty nonetheless. Her night-black hair had shone and glittered where now it hung limp and was brown from dirt, blood, and grime. Skin that had always been fair was now so pale beneath the second skin of dust she wore, it might have belonged to a ghost. Only her eyes remained to remind her captors who she was, eyes that had always been as hard and as cold as stone, narrowed into shards of ice. Kayneth did not answer her questions.

It had been a long time since she had felt as afraid as she did now. Faced with gods knew what ahead and this unknown stranger clamped to her arm, she really, truly didn't know what to expect. It had to have something to do with the Rainbow. That much was clear. The thought did not comfort her. The Rainbow wanted her dead – or as dead as the pledge allowed.

She opened her mouth to say something, perhaps to ask what was going on or who he was. Luckily, she was spared the embarrassment of choosing when their small party halted before a door. Neither large or small, the door did its job as well as any. It blocked the way forward and had to be hefted aside by two of her five guards.

She should really escape. It wouldn't even be that hard at the moment, with two of her guards preoccupied with the door. But . . . it had been forty-seven years since she had seen anyone from the Rainbow in any official capacity, not since she was caught and thrown into Trepidation. Maybe they had changed their mind about her sentence. She hadn't killed anyone who didn't deserve it. Her confirmed kills had either been political extremists or monsters.

The Rainbow killed monsters all the time. Her having killed one or twenty should have made no difference. So she decapitated a vampire and left its severed head at a shrine dedicated to the nature nymphs. No big deal. No harm done. Well . . . the nymphs had been mad, but apart from that . . .

Kayneth threw her forward, releasing his grip in time to send her sprawling onto the floor, her shackled feet rendering her otherwise impeccable balance useless. *No escape then. Right.*

She barked out a cry as her shoulder crunched against stone, ground her teeth deep into her tongue as her elbow popped and head clanged. Groaning, she spat blood, coughing past the retching iron taste seared permanently into her mind.

'Was that really necessary, Kayneth?' a new voice asked.

Yarra froze. Every muscle in her body, every blood vessel in her whole body simply seized up and ceased all movement.

Every single cell in Yarra's body stopped breathing. In the complete and utter silence that followed, the symphony of terrified screams, cracking whips, and mournful cries that was as much a common everyday occurrence as breathing drifted from the halls below.

She knew that voice, knew it, loved it, craved it, and had not heard it for so, so many years, not since she had run away and gotten herself thrown in the Halls of Trepidation. The man who had once been as close as a brother, whom she had not seen since her banishment more than seventy-five years ago, now stood over her and glared at Kayneth.

Ray Mossman.

2

Friends

S he didn't dare believe it, didn't dare look at him too closely.
'She should bow before you, Lord,' Kayneth said with mocking reverence.

'If she does not want to, she should not need to.'

Yarra kept her eyes down, her face hidden by her matted hair. Her mind whirred, spinning in overdrive, trying to make sense of this.

Rule One, she repeated to herself over and over like a mantra to centre herself. *Rule One.*

Aside from Ray, there were two others similarly attired. The three of them were clearly the leaders. Kayneth and the others who stood in the shadows clearly looked up to them, although they did so from behind reproachful glares.

Ray stood in the middle of their trio, his dark-brown hair covered by a hood not dissimilar to the one Kayneth wore. Ray's hood and the cloak shrouding the rest of him was green – but not the green of his eyes. Ray's eyes were a vibrant emerald. The figure to his left wore yellow so bright, it was almost gold. The one on the right wore red.

She didn't move, hardly dared to breath. How had they found her? Almost fifty years, she had been in the Halls of Trepidation, and no one had come looking for her. No one had come close to seeking her out or finding her.

How in all of Verstra had they found her? And why?

Ray looked almost the same as he had back then. There were no new lines across his face, and if he'd accumulated any more scars, they were hidden under that thick cloak. Despite the more than seventy years since their last meeting, his lack in changed appearance was not unexpected. They were immortal – or as close to it as any living being could be.

The vampires lived longer than they did, but as they were undead, Yarra didn't count them. Many of the demons too were truly immortal, but she didn't count them either; they were demons. Still, it was nice to see him again, despite the fact that his presence here most likely spelt her doom.

Rule One, she repeated to herself. *Rule One.*

'This is her then?' Ray asked, cool and calculated.

Yarra could practically feel Kayneth's gaze on her back.

'You tell me,' he spat. 'You know her best.'

Ray motioned with a single hand, and Kayneth hauled her to her feet. Wrists and legs shackled, she struggled to stand on her own. He grunted as he was forced to hold her up.

Rule One. Rule One.

Cold eyes glittered in triumph as his hood slipped free. Kayneth looked about the same age as Ray, although she vaguely remembered he was significantly older. He had a silver scar running vertical through the left side of his face, bisecting his eye and contorting his mouth into a permanent snarl. He had cherry gold hair that did little to soften his hard eyes.

'You're pretty,' she said, 'like a sunrise.'

'Well?' Kayneth snapped. 'Is there a way of telling who she is?'

The figure in red looked to the one in gold. Both looked to Ray, who gave them a subtle nod and a shrug.

'If I remember correctly, she had a scar on her right shoulder,' the one in red said.

'Claw marks,' the one in gold clarified.

Kayneth yanked at her collar. The tattered filthy dress she had worn almost for the entirety of her stay in Trepidation fell away from her too-thin form easily, leaving her bare before them. She shuffled from foot to foot, her chains rattling, completely naked before the three most powerful people in all of Verstra.

Rule One. Always follow Rule One.

'There's so much dirt,' Kayneth complained, peering at her back. Then he swore, 'Is this blood?'

'If I'd known the wolves were circling, I would have called off the hunt,' Yarra said, turning to show Ray her back. She was still thinking furiously. Rule One was to be held in utmost importance, always followed, never ignored until she knew more she would have to play it smart, bluff her way through. She was Yarra White, assassin and mercenary. She could do this. No problem.

'It's hard to tell,' Red Cloak said, 'but that could be claw marks.'

'Ignoring all the blood and dirt,' Gold Cloak said, cringing, 'there are lots of other scratches and scars. Can we be sure this is her?'

Yarra couldn't see his face, but she was sure Kayneth was glaring at her and that Ray was trying very hard to hide a smile. *So far, so good.*

'Send her back into the halls,' one of the people from the shadows said. 'If she is who you think she is, she'll escape.'

'Or not,' someone else said. 'Do not forget the very reason she might be in the halls in the first place.'

'Only someone extremely stupid would think the Halls of Trepidation were a good place to willingly go to,' Kayneth spat, kicking her viciously.

'Stupidity and brilliance often go hand in hand,' Yarra said, 'much like chocolate cake and mustard.'

Ray smiled again.

'Is there any way to be sure?' the voice from the shadows asked. 'Otherwise, all of this would have been for nothing.'

'There is a way,' Ray said.

All eyes turned to him.

'Have her name us.'

'Indeed,' Gold cloak said. 'If she is who we think, she will know us.'

A bone thrown by a friend would not go to waste.

Ray and his two companions took a step forward. The one in red held out a hand, and flames danced lightly around wavering fingers. Ray held his hand palm down, and the ground quivered. After a moment, the ground split, and a small sapling clawed into life, the only living thing inside the horrors of Trepidation. The third held out a hand, and a phantom wind blew the hoods away from all three faces.

Red Cloak had shoulder-length blond hair and piercing blue eyes; his face was tanned, and his eyes darted from Yarra to the shadowed figures behind him. Hands within easy reach of whatever weapons he had concealed beneath the cloak, his whole demeanour screamed danger and tension.

Ray was just Ray.

The golden-cloaked figure was female. She had eyes as gold as her cloak that burned with the fierce light of the sun. Her dark face was framed by darker curls.

'Do you know us?' Ray asked.

Not trusting herself to speak, Yarra only nodded. Bluffing time was over. Rule One was in full effect.

'This proves nothing,' Kayneth said. 'I bet a lot of people know who you are.'

Piercing blue eyes flashed dangerously.

'The lords of House Red, Green, and Yellow gather before the farmer, waiting for their tails to be chopped off.'

She'd almost forgotten how much fun it was to watch Ray struggle not to laugh.

'What is she talking about? Is she sane?'

Ray gave Kayneth a knowing smile. 'This is her.'

'You sure?'

'He's sure.'

Yarra snapped her shackles simply by pulling her wrists apart. Had she been anyone other than herself, such a feat would not have been possible; the solid iron shackles stifled any and all magic. She did the same with her legs. Not bothering to redress, she walked towards Ray without looking at him.

Stalked might have been a better word for it. She stalked towards him, placing each foot with over-exaggerated caution and precision. Rule One indeed. Let them see what the halls had done to her. Let them feel the pain of their failure.

'Ray is as sure as a tree that grows up towards the sun. Nice to see you again. By the way, Charlotte, the winds as wild as ever?' She stopped before the red-cloaked man and frowned. 'Ferric, long time no see, I guess. Whereas I perfected the art of being unreachable and fabulous . . . you got old.'

The four of them tilted their heads back and roared in laughter. But it was not true laughter. It was forced, borne of the situation they found themselves in. They still hated her; that was clear, even as all three of their faces grew tight with pain as they studied what she had become. This could still spell her doom – probably would.

'So am I to assume that this is all that remains of the originals? That our power has dwindled like that of evening rays bending before the darkness?' she asked.

'What are you saying?' Kayneth demanded, staring slack jawed in shock at the chains she had discarded like they were nothing more than cobwebs.

'There is an old saying,' Charlotte explained with a small half smile of her own. 'When one is dealing with a descendant of the White, one must always remember to ignore half of what is said.'

'Don't be mean, Charlotte.' Yarra pouted. 'I am not merely a descendant. I am the sole survivor of my family line, the inheritor of greatness, and the one with the weight of the world squarely on her shoulders.' She moved away from the trio, towards the shadowed people. 'I am the saviour. The survivor. The one feared far and wide by all those who oppose me. I am fire. I am death and health and light. I am –'

'*Yarra!*' Ray barked.

'I am sorry for overreacting.' She smiled. *Chalk up another win for Rule One.*

One of the shadowed figures could be heard muttering, 'Which half are we supposed to ignore?'

'So this is her. Can we go now?' Kayneth threw a fresh pair of shackles at her and stared her down.

Yarra reluctantly allowed herself to be shackled anew. These shackles were wooden, usually the worst material to make restraints out of, especially with Ferric so close by, but the wood was Rowan ash, and it was impervious to magic. It had the same effect on her the iron shackles had. Rule One was still in effect, but she was back to bluffing. There was nothing more she could learn from these people.

'Let's go.' Kayneth yanked on the chains.

Yarra stumbled after him, smirking at the shadowed figures and at Ray.

The three cloaked figures remained half a step behind them, muttering. They seemed to be having an argument, but Yarra couldn't hear what it was about. She could hazard a pretty good guess though. It appeared that despite the disquieting warmth of their first meeting in over seventy years, she was still not forgiven. They still hated her and wanted nothing to do with her or her family.

That was why Rule One was so important. It had kept her alive on more than one occasion, seen her emerge from certain death unscathed.

Rule One: always be the smartest one in the room.

If the enemy believed you knew as much as they did or more, they were exponentially less likely to kill you. Yarra had made that her philosophy. It had not saved her from the Rainbow or from Trepidation, but she would not let that stop her.

I am Yarra White, she told herself, *ruler of the Rainbow, and if they don't want me then they can go to hell.*

She was well within her rights to say that. She had been there and then fought her way out.

3

Chains

I t was decided that she would go to House Green with Ray as he was the only person willing to tolerate her presence for more than a few fleeting moments. And as he was one of the three remaining original families, the choice had always been among him, Ferric, or Charlotte anyway. Kayneth had handed over the chains that bound her and practically fled her presence.

It wasn't completely obvious if he knew who she was or not. Certainly, he had heard of her, probably heard of her unrivalled expertise and skill, the reputation she had been so careful to construct after the Rainbow disavowed her – but beyond that, her history and past, nothing. Rule One prevented her from asking why every single member of the Rainbow had travelled such a great distance just to break her out of prison. But she was sure to find out eventually. There were only so many situations that would warrant an act as large as that.

Ray hadn't travelled with any guards, which was strange, but then again, he was lord of House Green, and no one in their right mind would dare attack him. Still, protocol should have been followed. That it hadn't was . . . interesting. Something was definitely going on.

Kayneth had finally introduced himself as the leader of House Violet. Long-standing tradition prevented him from calling himself lord, but that was bound to change soon. The wheels had been set into motion long before the halls had claimed her. Just how far they had turned, she would need to find out. Soon.

Something deep inside her chest collapsed inwards, and she was filled suddenly with a profound deep sense of loss. Mummified in chains and dirt, all she could do was shuffle along behind Ray, not speaking, wallowing in this growing sense of hopelessness. If she was going to House Green again, nothing had changed. She was simply substituting one prison for another. Except this one, she wasn't walking into willingly.

'We'll camp here tonight,' Ray told her. 'Then we head home.'

The way he said that, 'home', made her shiver. It was a shiver that had nothing to do with the cold. The Halls of Trepidation was Verstra's largest prison, an impenetrable fortress of death and suffering guarded on all sides by the coldest and steepest mountains this land had to offer. The Maalia Mountains were dangerous at the best of times, at their peak, where the halls were; they were nothing short of lethal.

The Violet Lands were not as pretty as their name suggested. They were the most dangerous lands in all of Verstra, a title well earned thanks, in no small part, to the legendary death trap that was the Rubine Caves and the impenetrable fortress House Violet made its stronghold. The Maalia Mountains and the Halls of Trepidation just added to the lethality of the Violet Lands.

'We'll freeze,' Yarra said, teeth already rattling along with her chains. 'I'd rather go back inside. The halls are safer than this.'

Ray didn't smile, nor did he remove her chains or light a fire or set up any kind of camp, just settled down ten paces inside the halls and closed his eyes. Yarra was forced to do the same, her chains still clutched in his hands.

He clearly had not forgiven her then. Right.

The mystery of why Ray had no guards with him was solved the next morning when she woke with a stiff neck and indents of chains all over her body to find a small army surrounding her, glaring at her, dressed in the same green as Ray's cloak; it was immediately clear where their allegiance lay.

The person at their head was tall and dark with a messy shock of hair atop his head. His face was contorted in a sneer; his hand rested on his sword.

Yarra watched him from where she had slept on the ground, frost dusting her fingers and hair. Had there been an upside to sitting up and scowling, she was confident she would have, but as no upside could be found, she contented herself to watch him sideways from below.

'Royce,' Ray said tightly, 'this is a surprise.'

'It would not do to have you attacked, my lord,' the tall man said, 'especially with a condemned criminal in chains at your feet.'

Royce scowled down at her. She could practically read his intention to lash out and kick her in the side. She prepared herself for the impact.

'This is her, right? Not some imposter?'

'This is most definitely her,' Ray replied.

'You sure? She looks half dead, starved, and too weak to beat a kitten.'

'This is her,' Ray said, his tone leaving no room for further questions.

Royce bowed his head and made a series of quick hand movements that had the legions of armoured soldiers falling into formation. None of them offered to help her up, although all glared at her for not doing so. Ray, caught between scowling at Royce and muttering curses under his breath, did not stoop to help her either. Something had definitely changed.

Yarra lay there, waiting. Royce picked up the tail end of her chains and walked at the head of the heavily armed procession. Scores of men marched past where she lay, but still, she waited. She waited until her chains pulled tight, and she grunted against flesh that tore away. Still, she did not rise.

On and on, Royce walked, tugging the chain with all his considerable immortal might. Yarra did not say a word as she was dragged over rocks and roots, ice and cold that bit so deep, it burned, did not say a word as her chains caught and snagged, jerking her to violent and painful stops, did not cry out as her skin was rubbed raw and the drag marks behind her became streaked with blood, nor when her chains bit so deep, they buried themselves inside her and the streaks of blood turned into a torrent, staining the snow behind her crimson.

She put up with it all mutely, smiling slightly to herself.

4

Power

Royce had heard the rumours. Of course, he had heard the rumours. One did not be a part of the Rainbow without knowing at least part of its long and very bloody history. So he knew or at least suspected who she was. He just didn't believe it.

Of the seven great houses that governed and effectively ruled the world, he knew at least a little about all of them, from House Red and their elemental power over fire to the long-dead members of the ancient House Violet and the powers of shadow and darkness that died with them.

The Rainbow was comprised of those seven houses. Together, they protected the world from demons and monsters, vampires and werewolves and sirens and all kinds of unnatural beasts that sought to end their way of life and the world as they knew it.

The seven families that made up the Rainbow were well known. They were all powerful, all knowing. One could not travel anywhere in Verstra without crossing lands belonging to one of the Rainbow's houses. Yet there was one family that had ruled over them. In ancient times long past, there had been an eighth family of the Rainbow, the ruling family, although they had not ruled for centuries. That was the family he knew nothing about. That was the family shrouded in myth and rumour.

The family that ruled the Rainbow. The law all seven houses were held to.

The family the girl supposedly hailed from.

House White.

He knew nothing of them except they were supposedly more powerful than all the other houses combined. They'd have to be for all seven of the other houses to unquestioningly follow them. And that was why he didn't believe the girl was who she claimed.

There was no way any one with her level of power would allow herself to be dragged like cattle. There was no way someone as powerful as she would consent to being chained as she was, to be confined as he knew none of the lords could stand. She was shackled in Rowan ash, for god's sake. Her magic would be completely stifled; she was defenceless, powerless. There was no way the supposed leader of the Rainbow would allow herself to be treated in such a way.

Plus, she was a criminal, a murderer. The Rainbow was all that stood between the monsters and the whole of Verstra. The Rainbow stood for all that was good and righteous and right. There was no a chance in hell someone with as much blood on her hands as she had would be allowed to get anywhere near any of the Rainbow's key players, let alone lead them.

The fact that she was bleeding in a strong, steady torrent and still did not utter a sound further increased his irritation rather than convince him of her identity. She was probably too weak to cry out. He had encountered criminals released from Trepidation before. All had been broken husks. She no doubt was too. Whatever Lord Ray thought she could accomplish was not going to happen.

Nothing had been heard of House White in over seventy years. The last he had heard was the brutal murder of the lord and lady. Maybe this girl was a long-lost member of a branch family, one who had claim to the name but no real power. He was perfectly content to let her bleed to death.

Unfortunately, his underlings were becoming uneasy. Apparently, the sight of a chained girl being dragged unceremoniously behind an armed procession, trailing blood so thick, it coated the ground like paint, was not something they were comfortable seeing. *Oh well.*

He had spent at least a hundred years cultivating trust within the armies of House Green, many decades learning the ins and outs of Rainbow politics. He effectively ran House Green, although *Lord* Ray could never know the depth of mistrust he had festered within his guard. Even though he would have liked nothing more than to continue on their journey and let the girl die a slow painful death, he conceded the need to slow, then stop. He had to keep the soldiers' trust. It would raise issues if he were to be perceived as the type of person who ruthlessly let an injured girl bleed to death.

Night was coming, he rationalised. They needed to stop soon anyway.

Lord Ray sulked at the fringes of their party. Royce spared him a fleeting disgusted glance before he turned the same look to the girl. Some of his kinder-hearted men had helped her sit and were examining the chains, looking for a way to remove them. They had reached the tree line. The air here was slightly warmer, sparse trees providing shelter for their party. They were still in dangerous territory, still within the Violet Lands, where the forests were just as dangerous as the mountains.

'Do not unchain her!' he barked simply. 'Clean her wounds if you feel you must, but she will remain chained. We move out in ten minutes.'

'No,' Ray said simply. 'Break camp for the night. We'll resume in the morning.'

And because Ray was lord of House Green and Royce was not, the soldiers began setting up bedrolls and stoking small cooking fires.

Royce retreated a few steps, far enough away not to be noticed but close enough to hear the conversation that took place between the soldiers and the girl. Here, he could also keep a conspicuous eye on Ray. *Sorry, Lord Ray.*

'Why did you let him do this to you?' one of his soldiers asked, Zenon.

The girl blinked large unflinching eyes at him, unflinching as he placed a cloth over the half of her face distorted by scratches and dripping with blood, unflinching as another soldier dug deep into her sides and then arms and then legs, unearthing twigs and nuts and pebbles.

'To be one with the forest is all House Green has ever dreamed,' she said, gazing at Ray as if the soldiers around her did not exist.

'That's very deep, girlie,' Zenon said as he worked to heal her, his magic flashing softly.

'Yes, it is, isn't it?' she replied, turning her eyes to the scrapes and several deep gouges marring her body. 'Who are you?' she asked.

The soldier gave his name, but it was clear the girl wasn't listening. Her head was tilted back, and she was watching the clouds. Her hand, although pinned to her waist by the chains, traced the patterns she saw. When all her open wounds were cleaned, the splinters removed, and wounds healed as best Zenon could, the soldiers pulled her to her feet and held her as she swayed.

'We have to remove the chains!' the soldier called to him. 'We have to, Royce. They're killing her. Look.'

He saw Ray swing his gaze around to the girl in an instant, concern brimming from his eyes before he covered it with blank, annoyed disinterest. Royce narrowed his eyes and filed away this little morsel of information. There had to be something behind that, some meaning in the look they shared. Then he turned to the girl.

She was skeleton thin. The tattered clothes he assumed had before been covered in dirt and grime were now covered in blood, although she didn't seem to mind. The multitude of cuts and scrapes she had received had been cleaned of dirt and blood, but even healed, they were still glowing an angry red against her too-pale skin.

And the chains . . . the chains were almost enough to make him regret dragging her ruthlessly the way he had – almost.

The chains looked like they had been wrapped around her skeleton and then her skin layered on top. That was how deep they bit into her thighs and waist and chest and arms.

'Why?' Ray asked, his voice breaking a little over the word. In the fading light, his emerald eyes seemed to burn.

Royce started. He had not heard the lord's approach, had not seen him move. Despite the almost hundred years' experience he held over the young Ray Mossman, the youngster was still able to sneak up on him. It was probably because they were in the forest, surrounded by and immersed in earth, the Mossmans' trademark magical element.

'Why would you let it get that bad?'

The look the girl gave him was so tender, so full of love, the air seemed to crackle with it. Then ice slid over her eyes, and the moment was gone in an instant. *Interesting.*

'When one is treated like a criminal, one finds it easier to act like one than it is to convince others of one's innocence.' Stone-cold eyes shifted to the soldiers who hovered by her side, holding her upright. 'Who are you?' she asked.

'No one here thinks you're a criminal, Yarra,' Ray said softly, tenderly.

Royce's expression said otherwise, but Ray wasn't looking. The girl saw, saw the mistrust and disgust on his face and the faces of his soldiers and quirked her lips slightly to the side. It was not by any stretch of the imagination a smile, more a grimace or a slight vicious bearing of teeth.

'I am here to help,' she said. 'You wouldn't have found me if I hadn't wanted you to, and I could escape any time I want. You are all alive because I am curious what I could do for the Rainbow after all this time. Should I want it, you'd all be dead like . . . that.'

She snapped her fingers, not even so much as flinching as the movement grated the chains deeper into her flesh and a fresh wave of blood warmed her too-pale skin.

Royce frowned, his hand drifting suspiciously towards his sword. Although the words weren't said as a threat, the cold, hard glint in her eyes suggested otherwise, and there was something about the way Ray held himself, something about his sudden stillness, the way his hand simply froze mid-air as he reached for her shoulder, the pain etched across his face, gave him pause.

'Yarra . . .,' Ray said, his voice almost a sob and a plea. 'Please.'

The girl simply lay down to sleep, folding her chained legs neatly under her and manoeuvring her body down onto the ground, face turning away from Ray and the soldiers, eyes closing. Royce couldn't tell if she slept, but she did not move.

He checked every hour. Royce checked that she had not escaped, looked over to her chained form to see it unchanged and unmoving. Only once in the night did she move, to roll over and face the darkened sky. She gazed up at the stars and the clouds that waltzed across the heavens. Even in the darkness, broken by a single one of their small fires, he could see her silver eyes shine.

Her chin was still tilted up as the sun rose. She did not move as the soldiers resumed their marching. Royce faced her, thoughts of dragging her the rest of the way haunting him as a phantom ache in his well-developed arms. Then he tossed her chains to the nearest soldier and strode off without a backwards glance. *Let the underlings deal with her.*

They would either drag her themselves, carry her like the dead weight she was, or risk his wrath by releasing her, and in all honesty, he found he truly didn't care.

5

Trouble

Nestled at the base of the great Maalia Mountains and spanning many more miles outwards the Ashdown Forest was a sight for sore eyes and a welcome end to the harsh cold of the mountains. They trekked for two days down the rolling forest slopes before the ground levelled out into gentle hills. The transition from the Violet Lands to the Lands of Green was marked by a single pillar-like stone. It was an unremarkable stone to any who didn't know what to look for. Tall and pale, the stone was clearly not natural. On the side of the Violet Lands was a small carved cauldron, on the side of the Green Lands a similarly carved tree.

The marker stone was not the only indication that they had left the Violet Lands. The atmosphere changed almost immediately. The forest suddenly seemed calmer, less imposing – friendly, almost. Three days after that, the trees thinned, and houses could be seen amongst the forest greenery. A day after that, their destination was in sight.

House Green crested the horizon like a great morning star banishing the darkness of the night. Its great towers reached for the sky, seeking to hold the weight of the world and to protect the ancient-looking rectangular library between them. Wrought-iron gates stood to attention, flanked by topiary thorn bushes depicting gargoyles and fanged beasts.

The headquarters of House Green: Ivy Library.

Yarra had allowed herself to be carried like a child, had put up with it without complaint for hours upon hours. Had allowed them to treat her like a child whenever they made camp, allowed them to feed her, to bathe her, and to clean her wounds, never complaining or saying a word against them, even as the chains bit deeper and deeper into her flesh and her bones jolted at each and every step the soldier took.

She was an assassin. She was used to waiting patiently. She could wait for hours, days, weeks if need be, years if the situation called for it. It was a learned skill; patience had not come naturally to her. But she had had decades to practice. She had gotten very good. She could be very, very patient.

All that melted away the moment the large and ominous building appeared on the horizon.

She sat bolt upright in the soldier's arms, ignoring his barked cry of alarm first at her movement and then at the torrent of blood it caused to cascade over his arms.

'*Raaaay!*' she screamed, surging forward and lurching out of the arms that clutched at her.

Free from the soldier but not the chains, she fell hard to the ground. Even then, she did not stop. Struggling forward, inching along the ground like a caterpillar, she raged against the chains, shouting all the way. This was bad.

It seemed like an age before Ray appeared before her, crouching in the dirt, his face drawn, taught and pale. Hands on her shoulders, he hauled her up. If he was aware of the pain this caused her, he didn't show it, probably aware that it didn't bother her in the slightest. Bad, bad, very bad.

'What is it?' he demanded near, shaking her in his haste.

Yarra opened her mouth and was forced to spit out a mouthful of blood before she could speak.

'No riddles, Yarra,' Ray said, 'please.'

Stone-cold eyes flashed in amusement, and she shut her mouth, swallowed, and then met his gaze.

'Permission to speak freely, Lord?' she asked.

Well aware of all ears listening in and of Royce, hovering close by, very interested in what was being said, Ray nodded.

'Am I your prisoner?' she asked.

'No.'

'Have I been bound?'

'No.'

Yarra blinked, the only sign she showed of her shock, and then frowned. 'I really should have been bound. Why wasn't I bound? I could run, you know. This could all be a hoax to get you to release me. It wouldn't be the first time. I am an escape artist, you know.'

'Yarra . . .,' Ray urged.

Right. Emergency. 'Do you love me?'

There was a tightness in her chest that had nothing to do with the hitch in her breath and sudden pain in the emerald eyes that met hers.

'No.'

'Do you trust me?'

Ray did not meet her eyes, head bowed in what could only have been perceived as defeat. She waited, needing to hear the answer as much as the soldiers around her.

'Yes. Yes, Yarra, of course, I trust you. I will always trust you.'

She closed her eyes, let the words wash over her, and loosed a shuddering breath that sent shockwaves of pain and blood rippling through her. Eyes still closed, she started speaking, softly and quickly.

The soldiers and Royce could hear nothing of what she said, but the effect of her words was evident in his face. Devastation and fear warred with each other for dominance in his features. His mouth gaped and eyes shone silver. He gulped.

'Your presence would endanger them further,' he said tightly.

'They will die without me.'

'You are in no state to fight.'

'I won't know that until I try.'

'You could die.'

Yarra tunnelled deep inside herself, dredging up the last vestiges of her power. 'So could you.'

Ray hung his head, defeat and desperation etched across every line of his body.

'Go,' he rasped out. 'Go . . . please.'

Yarra dipped her head and folded into shadow, not completely but enough to slip through the chains, to step from them like they were nothing more than cobwebs to be brushed lightly aside, exactly like she had done with the shackles in Trepidation.

The deep gauges remaining in her arms, legs, and torso were painfully visible, but she took a step forward and then another until she was running, running through the scores of soldiers who were powerless to stop her.

Crouched on the ground in mute shock, Ray remained stunned. He fought back panic and fear and relief, relief that Yarra was here, that she would help, that all was not lost as long as she was here, fear that she may be injured further, that even though she said she would help, she might not. She was a criminal, a liar. Her word could not be trusted. And yet . . .

'My lord?' Zenon asked.

'Lord Mossman,' Royce said, his voice hard, 'we cannot allow that criminal to run free. She must be caught immediately.'

Ray took a deep breath. When he spoke, his voice was firm, the voice of a lord speaking to his soldiers and allowing no room for argument.

'She is not a criminal,' he said. 'We move. Now. Royce, I want a dozen of your best fighters to leave immediately for Ivy. As soon as you are able, I want everyone else to follow. Be prepared to fight your way in and kill on sight.'

Not a sound from the soldiers. Not a whispered question or muttered curse. Complete and utter all-consuming silence. But beneath that silence, there was confusion, confusion as to why their lord would release the prisoner. Why would he set her free and then insist she was not a criminal? The girl had been dragged from Trepidation in chains. Her status as a criminal was assured and irrevocable, so why was their lord insisting otherwise?

Under the confusion, there was fear, fear that their lord was going mad, that the stress of ruling House Green, a powerful member of the Rainbow, was finally starting to show. Beneath the fear: doubt and mistrust.

'What is it, my lord?' Royce asked.

'Werewolves have attacked the library,' he said softly but not weakly. 'They have breached our defences and infiltrated our home and cannot be allowed to succeed in whatever foul mischief they are plotting.'

'How do you know?' Royce asked.

There was indecision in Ray's emerald eyes, like he was trying to decide what to say – or if he should say anything at all.

'Yarra is . . . special,' Ray said at last. 'Her magic is . . . different. Special.' Ray glanced around, casting his eyes around, looking for something to latch onto, something to save him from having to say more. He found nothing.

'Yarra is a seer,' he said at last, throwing his hands out in defeat. 'She can see the future – or pieces of it. Flashes, really. Sometimes they get muddled up. That's why one must always remember to ignore half of what is said. She gets confused. But . . . she . . . she saw their deaths.'

His family. The siblings he had left back at Ivy. Dead. Slaughtered.

Royce saw the hard glint in Ray's eyes and made a decision. Barking orders to the soldiers faster than they had any hope of listening to, he rallied them and sent his fastest hurtling towards House Green.

Despite his ambition and his dislike for Ray and the Mossman family, he felt a pang of fear at the thought of the youngest – sweet, young Annika – facing such creatures alone. And despite himself, he found himself hoping the girl was who she claimed and that her power was as potent as legend suggested.

6

Werewolves

Yarra was sure she was screaming, was sure her lungs and legs would give out at any time, but she did not care, did not care that one falter could spell the end for her and the people she loved more than her own family, whom she loved so much more than she loved herself, whose lives she valued far above her own.

So she screamed and pushed her body past its limits and sprinted for all she was worth towards the library.

She did not stop to heal herself, to seal the deep, persistently bleeding chain marks across her body. Healing would take time she did not want to lose. The soldiers had done an adequate job healing her. Zenon was a good a healer as any, not on the Dijon scale but good nonetheless; that would have to be enough. It would take time too to open the wrought-iron gates, so she scaled them, climbing nimbly up the gate, vaulting over the spikes, and landing lightly before sprinting off again.

It was perhaps a miracle she could perform such acrobatic feats after Trepidation. But although most all her fifty years there had been spent in chains, she had not allowed herself to go soft. That was Rule Four – more or less.

Where Rule One ensured she was always intellectually ahead of any adversary she might face, Rule Four ensured she was always – and never – underestimated, always because she was a girl and relatively young and slight in stature and build, never because her eyes always gave her away or the way she walked or the way she held herself. There was always something the bad guys picked up on that gave her away.

But Rule Four could go one of two ways and often went both at once, so it hardly mattered.

She pelted up the tiered steps, lunged through the open and fractured door.

Bodies greeted her entrance, bodies of guards dressed in green now turned brown with their blood, bodies torn apart by taloned hands, heads ripped from necks, arms and legs shredded, abdomens sliced open.

There were no survivors.

She paused for a moment by a cluster of trees – unremarkable save for the fact that they grew inside with vicious, wickedly sharp, and unnaturally long spines that skewered the furry grey of the werewolves' hide, pinning them in place.

The moment's pause was to admire the skill it had no doubt taken to grow the plants fast enough to skewer the intruders. Then she was off again, hurtling towards the faint sounds of battle, towards the screams and unearthly howls.

Her heart breaking in two.

She stopped just once more, just once, to grab the only weapon she could find: a small knife with a blade the length of her palm. *Rule Four.* Then Yarra White launched her exhausted and broken body into battle.

She went undetected for a full five seconds before the werewolves' superior sense of smell alerted them to her presence and three charged at her. Those first five seconds were used to implement Rule Four, part one: always be underestimated.

The first second was used to survey the wreckage, the large hall that had been the dining room, now utterly destroyed, and the large table overturned and wrecked.

One second was dedicated to counting the werewolves, learning their positions, which were injured and which needed to die first.

Two seconds were spent cataloguing survivors of House Green, finding those precious souls in the sea of snarling bodies, two boys and two girls fighting with all their gods-given might, fighting with that elemental power they had been given and the decades of training drilled into each and every one of them from the day they took their first steps.

The final second was spent contemplating just how stupid it would be to charge unarmed into a warring pack of werewolves. The rational part of her, the part that knew this was stupid and that she would most likely die if she attempted this, screamed at her to stop. She charged ahead regardless. That voice had never held credence with her.

What would it matter if she died anyway? The world would go on without her in it. Besides, after Trepidation, some action would be welcomed.

Royce had claimed she was out of shape. Perhaps he was right. Perhaps not. Whatever the case, she was about to find. Rule Four, part two.

She took the first few face on. As they turned to attack her, she met them, driving her small knife into the face of the first and then ducking under the second and striking the third in the face with her fist. Now she really did face a room full of werewolves unarmed. *Oops.*

The werewolves were half a metre larger than your average-sized immortal, and Yarra was on the shorter side. To her, the werewolves were huge, massive monsters. Yet she tackled one like a star sportsman, toppling it onto the floor and all but collapsing on top of it.

Panting, she wiped sweat and blood from her eyes, hacked a glob of blood onto the werewolf, and groaned, loud and long.

Maybe she was out of shape, really, badly out of shape – fatally out of shape, even. *Maybe.*

Her chain marks leaked blood, and as the wounds were still open, the werewolves hardly had to do anything to get their filthy, mud-coated claws inside of her, which hurt.

But the hurt was good. After Trepidation, it was even welcomed. The pain sent heat through her limbs, sent fire rushing through her veins, burning her from the inside out, warming her against the bitter freeze Trepidation had seared into her soul for all those years.

She whirlwinded through them, kicking and punching with one goal in mind, one clear goal in sight, and she didn't care if she killed herself to achieve it.

For all the Mossmans had done for her, for all they had done for the broken little girl with no one and nothing to love, for all Ray had done for her, for the love he had given a loveless child and the family his family had become, for the life they had convinced her was worth living and for the scars they had healed, for the unending and unrelenting love they had for one another, for their future, she would save them. She had to save them.

Nothing would stop her, not the five werewolves all consumed with ripping the girl apart or the frantic boy failing to tear them away.

No no no no no no.

'Matt!' she barked, voice cracking slightly. 'Move.'

The skinny youth with a mess of creamy mahogany hair and fear-stricken, pain-filled emerald eyes turned instinctively towards her voice. His eyes widened as he saw her. He sprang away, tossing a curled whip-like item towards her. Yarra caught it without looking, but her eyes sparkled as she recognised the feel of the leather.

That put Rule Five firmly into play. Oh, this would be fun for her.

Rule Five was simple. It demanded revenge.

It was her weapon, the weapon she hadn't seen hide nor hair of since she ran. Myrthos was its name, the flexible rapier hidden inside a nondescript double-barred whip, Her pride and joy.

'Oh-ho, now you're in for it,' she said softly, 'I'll make you pay for hurting Kelly.'

Her heart demanded it.

7

Panic

Ray's panic was so tangible, so obviously all-consuming that Royce was tempted to let him off the hook, to temporarily take a step back from his ever-pressing takeover plans and actually act like a loyal and devoted captain of the guard. But he couldn't do that. He couldn't show even the smallest morsel of weakness or sympathy towards his lord, else he risked losing the fragile trust he had built. A shame, that.

'Can't we go any faster?' Ray asked.

'We're pushing forward as fast as we can, Lord,' one soldier replied, panting.

'They could be hurt or, or dying or . . . or worse.'

There was no need to ask whom he was worried about. They all knew who he had left behind to guard their fortress stronghold. They all knew what he would sacrifice to save them, to keep them from harm, the siblings he valued more than his own life.

What could be worse than losing the family he so obviously loved so much? What could be worse than knowing your family was fighting tooth and claw against werewolves who had invaded their home?

What could be so much worse? It was causing a thick sheen of sweat to form on his brow, soak through his hair, and fling like stray raindrops across the ground as he rushed towards his home.

'Faster,' Ray muttered. 'Faster, faster, faster.'

There was clearly a reason he was so agitated, definitely interesting – potential blackmail material, anything to further his takeover movement.

Their lord increased his pace, and the soldiers gradually fell behind. Royce kept pace with him easily, not speaking or judging, just silently providing support, using his own magic to keep up, magic that gave him swiftness and speed, thinking. That was his role in situations such as these, to provide support for the lord he hated and would replace as soon as he could. If the deaths of the Mossman siblings took him closer to his goal, then he could live with that, even if it meant sacrificing dear, sweet little Annika.

He personally could think of nothing worse than to lose one's whole family. But who was he to judge the priorities of one of the seven lords? They were law unto themselves. Anything they wanted, they got. They could do whatever they wanted without consequence. He had known lords of other houses to go on violent massacres and slaughter entire civilisations on a whim. How was he to know if family even meant a damn to them?

But Royce did know. He did know that Ray loved his sisters and brothers more than he valued his own life. He knew that Ray was one of the most loving, caring individuals he had ever met. It didn't matter that Ray was lord of House Green, blessed with the strongest of elemental earth magic; he loved his siblings with fierceness akin to that of a dragon protecting its hoard, with the strength of a raging fire or the unstoppable force of a river in flood.

'No, no, no, no, no,' he moaned, pushing himself faster.

Royce could do nothing but stare after the lord as he forged ahead, heedless of the trees and branches and rocks in his path, hurtling over them with speed that suggested he was blessed with power over air rather than earth, even as the very earth beneath them, the trees and leaves and bushes, every aspect of the Ashdown Forest, seemed to urge him forward faster and faster and faster.

'He's not going to stop, is he, Captain?' Zenon asked through panted, rasping breaths.

Royce snorted. 'Doubt it.'

'What do we do?'

'follow as fast as you can. I'll go with him, see if I can't defuse the situation before you get there.'

Zenon saluted with a sharp 'Sir'.

So Royce tore after the lord, fixing his eyes on the tail end of his green cloak, and ran.

Wrought-iron gates swung on rusty hinges, thrown open as Ray sprinted past. He bounded up the steps and was gone.

Royce slowed to a walk the moment he reached the iron fence, mere moments after Ray. There was no noise from within the library. Whatever had happened had happened. There was no more fighting to be done. Those who had died would remain dead. The werewolves had either been slaughtered or the slaughterers, and there was nothing he or Ray could do about that now.

So Royce walked up the steps, noting the blood that spattered over them and the gouges in the door, walked along the hall, noting the bodies that greeted him, the clusters of speedily grown branches and the werewolves they impaled, walked past the ruined rooms filled with tattered furniture, mangled bodies, and destruction on a level he had not seen since the last war.

There was nothing to suggest the girl had passed this way, nothing to suggest she had not taken her chances and run. If she had attempted escape, he could pin it on Ray, present Ray as incompetent before the convergence of other lords and leaders, have him removed from power that way. It was worth a try. Hell, it might even work.

He kept walking until he reached the remnants of the dining room. When he stopped, it was not because he had reached his destination, nor was it because the destruction contained inside that room was so great, it looked like a cyclone had swept through. It was not the number of werewolf bodies that stopped him or the gruesome nature of some of the corpses.

House Red might be feared and famed as the warriors of the Rainbow, the most fearsome and skilled fighters, but this . . . this was a good and timely reminder that House Green was not to be trifled with, that they too were warriors. This was why he had been planning his takeover for so painstakingly long: to be sure it worked so he wouldn't end up like this.

There were only five figures who remained, five people in all, five people who clutched at one another and clung together like their lives depended on it. That was the feeling he got from looking at their group and a sixth figure standing separate, head bowed, arms wringing in frustration, anger, sadness, and fear.

'Lord Ray?' Royce asked softly, tentatively.

The solitary figure did not stir. The huddled group of figures made no move. Royce wisely decided to keep his mouth shut. He watched, monitoring every move, listening to every word, filing away every little piece of information handed to him for further use – listening, watching, learning, planning.

'A-Annika . . . a-are you OK?' Ray asked in what was scarcely more than a whisper, his voice shaking.

Annika was scarcely thirty, a child by their immortal standards. She had true pure mahogany-brown hair bound in pigtails atop her head, tied with pink blood-splattered bows. Her smooth blood-flecked face turned briefly towards her brother; her emerald eyes, although shining, were hard.

'How could you?' she said softly but with a harshness that did not suit her. 'How could you let this happen?'

Ray failed to hold her stare, and she turned away in disgust, turned away from her brother and crouched down beside the two on the ground.

'Erryk . . .,' Ray said, his voice breaking, the hand he had outstretched falling limply to his side. 'I'm sorry.'

Erryk, heir to House Green, cast a grieving look over his siblings and then to his elder brother. There was sadness in his voice and sorrow, but it did not sound like he blamed his brother the way Annika did.

'She protected us,' he said. 'She saved us. Saved us even though all you've ever done, all we've ever done, is scorn and condemn her.'

'I know,' Ray said, his voice breaking completely. 'I know.'

He swallowed, visibly choking back tears. His hands shook so much, he fisted them at his sides to stop the movement, spooling in the rage and fear and pain he felt, enclosing them inside him.

Twin pairs of emerald eyes met across the carnage, and Erryk, although younger, seemed suddenly to shoulder more responsibility. Where Ray hung his head, Erryk held his high, his slightly curly hair weighed down by the blood of his enemies, even as his own blood trickled from a wound on his temple.

If a Mossman had to rule House Green, Royce would have preferred it to have been Erryk.

'We all live because of her,' Erryk said.

'H-how is she?'

The warmth that might have started seeping into Erryk's eyes was instantly gone. 'Do you really have the right to ask that?' he asked, all emotion instantly lost, 'to ask about her well-being over that of one of your own?'

Ray instantly froze.

Erryk gave a low, humourless laugh. 'I said we all lived, didn't I? I didn't say we got away unscathed.'

Erryk stepped aside as Ray approached, revealing the two figures on the ground. Annika stood and glared at Ray, nothing but hate in her gaze. Erryk pulled her to him, away from Ray as Ray took in the sight before him.

Two figures lay side by side. *Broken* was the only word that sprung to mind at the sight of her.

Hair that was more golden than her sisters' had been dyed near black with blood. Her face, a face that had smiled both kindly and fiercely, had been ruined, split from the corner of her mouth right up to under her ear on the right. Her right arm had been shattered, her left mauled. It looked like one of the werewolves had bitten her side and shook her like a doll. Similar bite marks marred her legs, and Ray couldn't help but think the werewolves had enjoyed attempting to rip her apart.

There was no spark of life in those brilliant half-closed emerald eyes. Erryk had said they were all alive; she had to be alive too. She had to live, had to. And . . . yes. There it was. The rise and fall of her chest, however slight, was there, and as long as it remained, there was chance for recovery.

'Kelly . . .,' he said softly, brokenly stroking a finger down her face, 'what did they do to you?'

'She saved me.'

Ray turned to the second figure lying on the ground, a lad with creamier mahogany hair he refused to style and an unnatural ability to remain completely still. Silent tears streamed down his face. Although his injuries were nowhere near as severe as hers, he lay beside her, providing support and comfort, as he always had done and always would do.

'They were going to get me, would have killed me, but she got in the way. She antagonised them into attacking her. She bought me time to run, to get away. And when they were . . . when they were tearing at her . . . tearing at her like she was a toy . . . I could do nothing. Nothing. I tried. I tried. I fought them. I tried . . .'

Ray laid a hand over his, gave it a firm squeeze. 'I'm sure you did, Matt. I'm sure you did everything you could to save her.'

Finally, Ray dragged his eyes over to the girl, to Yarra. She was standing, bloodied and battered, panting but alive, surveying the injured Mossmans with the same amount of love and tenderness Ray had shown. She wobbled where she stood, black blood mingling with the red that spilled from her.

'I . . .,' she said before pitching forward, limbs going slack and eyes rolling up in her head.

Ray was moving before she hit the ground, scooping her up in his arms, holding her tight, his face gaunt and pale. *Interesting.*

Had he not known better, he would have said she had been gutted. Scratches marred every inch of her, many crusted with dirt, and her midnight hair no more than a pool of blood around her head. But Ray knew the gouges across her stomach, arms, and legs were from chains pulled too tight. Beside her, like it had fallen from her grasp, was a curled whip, its tip shining. Bloodless lips opened as she panted short shallow breaths, fighting to keep her conscious despite the darkness that threatened to pull her under.

Eyes that had held love and tenderness now showed anger and rage and fear, so much fear.

'What happened?' Ray demanded of his siblings. '*What happened?*'

8

Hero

Royce made sure he remained with the family until the rest of his men arrived; then he instructed them to carry Kelly, Matt, and the girl to the infirmary – carefully. Even then, he did not stray far from Ray's side – all part of the act.

That was his place, to be by his lord's side should he need anything, to be there to protect him, to offer advice or to weather the storm of emotions brewing behind his eyes. It did not matter that the Mossmans were not fit to lead House Green in the future; for the moment, he was there to support, nothing more, an act. The Rainbow must remain strong.

'What happened?' Ray demanded the moment Kelly's condition was pronounced stable and the rest of his siblings had been seen to their various wounds, patched up and wrapped with bandages. The girl's condition remained a mystery, but Ray didn't seem as concerned as he had been, so Royce put it out of his mind. Zenon had probably healed her, was probably still working his small gift of healing magic on all the wounded.

'They just attacked,' Annika said, 'attacked us for no reason like the monsters they are.'

'No, Annika,' Erryk said gently. 'They did have a reason. Did you forget we wiped out that entire pack last month?'

'That's no excuse!' she snapped.

'They walked in here like the wards meant nothing,' Erryk said, facing his elder brother again. 'Once inside, they slaughtered the guards you left behind in an instant. Then they came for us.'

'I didn't . . .' Ray stopped, his eyes flicking to Royce beside him. 'Then what happened?'

'We fought them,' Matt said, sitting still as stone on the edge of Kelly's bed, fingers interlaced with his twins. 'We were even winning.'

Ray smiled, remembering the werewolves impaled in the hastily grown branches and the trail of bodies leading to the dining room he had found them in. Considering the number of werewolves dead, this must have been a large pack; that, or two packs had joined forces to attack House Green at its most vulnerable: when their lord had been away, when Ray had been away. Interesting.

And bad – very bad. It suggested the werewolves had inside information on the workings of House Green, especially if the wards had been disabled.

'Winning,' Erryk echoed, 'until we weren't. They just kept coming. More and more of them rushing through the doors, pushing past the injured and dying to get to us. The dining room was our last defence. If they had to be allowed to roam free in our home, we could at least keep them away from the books. They had us outnumbered, but we fought. We'd seen a few werewolves with what looked like dirt on their claws. When they scratched someone, even if it was another werewolf, they went down and did not get back up.'

'We assumed poison,' Annika said.

Erryk nodded. 'We avoided those ones as best we could, but we were losing ground. Then Matt was cornered, and Kelly was surrounded, and Yarra . . . she saved us.'

The girl, Yarra, had been half dead when she had taken off from their party, running for all she was worth. Royce considered the fact that he might have to reconsider his assessment of her. Clearly, she had made it here in no time at all. Clearly, she had had enough strength to fight off a considerable number of werewolves, enough for the Mossman brats to seize victory. Maybe she was as powerful as the rumours claimed, even if she had at last succumbed to unconsciousness, although whether from blood loss, exhaustion, or the mysterious poison on the werewolves' claws, he did not know.

He hoped poison. That way, there was a chance she might not wake up.

'Tell me what happened,' Ray said, moving closer to Matt. Erryk opened his mouth, but Ray shook his head. 'I want to hear it from you.'

Unblinking eyes never left his sister's face, but Matt began to speak.

'I fell,' he said. 'I ducked under one of the poisoned werewolves and had to jump onto the table to dodge a second, but I landed on one of the plates. It broke, and I fell. I dropped my sword, hit my hand on a chair.' Matt lifted his bandaged wrist slightly. 'The werewolves, well, they didn't care if they destroyed the table or broke the plates. They even threw one at me. It hit me in the face here. I screamed, and they laughed at me. Then there was one in front of me, holding my sword, pointing *my* sword at my chest, and there was nothing I could do.'

Tears began falling down his face, but he made no move to wipe them away. The cut on his temple, although sealed, still looked angry and red. Ray placed a hand on his shoulder.

'He was going to stab me. He was going to kill me. But . . . but Kelly got it first. She stabbed it before it could stab me. Then she taunted them, called them crybabies, even though I was the one crying. She called them "cute little fluffy puppies" and insulted their mothers, and they all went after her. She told me to run, to grab my sword and to run, but I couldn't. I was too scared. Even when they grabbed her, she was telling me to run. She let them catch her so they wouldn't get to me, and they knew it. Three of them bit her. A fourth declared a competition to see who could rip off the biggest chunk. And she screamed. She screamed for me to run, to get away, to be safe. And I couldn't do anything.'

'That's not true,' Annika said. 'You fought. You should have seen him,' she said with sudden conviction, near snarling through her teeth. 'He fought them. Even as the others made a wall around her, he fought them.'

'But I couldn't do anything,' Matt said, tears coming thick and fast. 'I couldn't save her.'

'You did,' Annika said firmly. 'If you hadn't given Yarra Myrthos, she wouldn't have been able to save Kelly. You did that, Matt, you.'

'Myrthos,' Ray said. 'I didn't know you had that, Matt.'

'I always carry it,' Matt said with a touch of pride in his voice, 'in case she ever came back.'

Four sets of emerald eyes drifted across to the other bed and the girl slumbering beneath the sheets.

'What did she do?' Ray asked. 'Did she use the move?'

Erryk laughed slightly.

Even Matt cracked a grin. 'No, nothing quite as outrageous as that.'

'That explains why Myrthos was still in its whip form then,' Ray said.

Erryk nodded. 'Indeed.'

Royce hoped he didn't look as confused as he felt. He had never heard of Myrthos, and he had been affiliated with the Rainbow for centuries. He thought he knew everything there was to know about House Green in particular, yet from this brief conversation alone, he was learning more than he had these past fifty years.

And speaking of these past fifty years, how was it that Annika spoke of the girl with the same familiarity Ray did? Annika spoke of Yarra like a friend. Or a sister . . . or saviour. How was it that Annika knew her in the first place? Annika was scarcely thirty years old. The girl had been trapped in the Halls of Trepidation for the past fifty. There was no way they could have met. No way.

'What exactly did she do?' Ray asked again.

Erryk smiled. 'Let's just say she went a little crazy.'

'Nothing they didn't deserve,' Annika spat.

'Indeed,' Erryk agreed, 'but still . . . the werewolves had formed a wall between us and where they were ripping up Kelly. Matt was trying to get past them when Yarra arrived. As soon as he saw her, he passed her Myrthos. Then she went over, actually over, the werewolf wall.'

'Dived over it, more like,' Annika added with glee.

'Dived over it then,' Erryk amended. 'She wrapped the whip around the throat of one of the werewolves biting Kelly and threw it, actually threw it, into the backs of the ones creating the wall. The werewolves dropped Kelly and pounced on her.'

'She jumped on the shoulders of this big gruff-looking one and rode him like a bull,' Annika added enthusiastically.

'It was like she was dancing,' Matt said. 'Every move brought one of them down or hurt one in some way. There was no wasted effort on her part. It was beautiful.'

'There is nothing beautiful in slaughter, Matt,' Ray said. Something in Matt's face fell, and he hastily added, 'Although I do know what you mean.'

'A lot can be learned from watching a master dance,' Erryk said. 'Unfortunately, when one is paired with a hopeless partner, accidents tend to happen. We tried, Ray. Really, we did, but numbers were not on our side, and well . . .'

Again, emerald eyes turned to where Yarra slept.

'She was scratched,' Annika said bluntly in answer to Ray's unasked question, 'and bitten, I think. I didn't see it.'

Annika rubbed at her own arm, in the place where Yarra's arm was bandaged. Her emerald eyes were haunted, that same haunted look reflected in all the Mossmans' eyes. *Curious.*

'She went down, but then she got up. By that time, there were only a few of them left, all injured, and Annika and I were able to finish them off,' Erryk said. 'It must have been one of the ones with poisoned claws that got her. Ray, I'm sorry. We failed.'

Royce did not understand the despairing look Erryk gave his brother or the fear that suddenly flashed through Annika's and turned Matt's face pale. More secrets, more things to uncover and wield as weapons against them. They all looked genuinely afraid. What could have caused them to be so afraid?

Ray merely smiled and looked over at Yarra again. He sighed. 'Poison, was it? That's what it took for you finally to keel over? Really, Yarra, how long were you planning on resting this time?'

Royce and everyone else – for indeed, all of Ray's siblings were looking on with just as much shock as he was – gaped as Yarra cracked open an eye, stone-cold irises glimmering in amusement and annoyance.

'Damn you, Ray,' she croaked weakly. 'Any other lord would have killed them by now. You always knew how to surprise me. Damn you for knowing me too well and spoiling all my fun.'

'How long were you unconscious because of the poison, and how long were you just sleeping?' Ray demanded, a smile dancing about his lips.

'Well, let's see . . .,' Yarra said, struggling to force herself into a sitting position and failing. 'First, there was the initial poisoning, and then there were those other two that tried to eat me, but then they were dead, and I thought this would be the perfect time for a nice long nap. Unfortunately, naps are not in the cards, and we lost far more than we won today anyway. With the loss of another primary from the ranks, we find ourselves severely short staffed.'

Royce did not have a clue what she was rambling on about, and again, he was visited by the unwelcome feeling that he had misjudged her. It made him very uneasy, and he did not like it one bit. The Mossmans, however, shared a knowing look that set his teeth on edge. Was this what Ray meant when he said one must always remember to ignore half of what is said?

Ray levelled the girl with a hard stare.

'Considering I had not slept in days, had been practically dragged through hell, was bleeding quite heavily, I might add, and then sprinted all the way here without rest, not to mention the three werewolves I literally had to tear off Kelly to stop them eating her, the seven I then fought off to protect Matt before slaughtering another five or so that were trying to disembowel Annika, oh, and don't forget the past fifty years I spent chained in Trepidation –'

'How long?' Ray demanded.

Despite her injuries and obvious exhaustion, she managed to pull off a specular pout. 'About two minutes, I think,' she said without batting an eye.

As his siblings barked out laughs that were quickly covered by coughs, Ray only stared at her. He blinked once, very slowly.

'Two minutes,' he said. 'You're slipping.'

There was nothing mortal in the grin she flashed at him, the glimmer of teeth and eyes far too hard.

Royce shivered, unable to stop himself. What was she? What had she endured to be able to joke so easily about what would have been certain death for anyone else?

And more importantly, how the hell was she still alive?

9

Questions

Royce thought he was ready to assume leadership of House Green. He had plotted and schemed and wormed his way into the Rainbow. He was ready to carry on the legacy of House Green just as soon as Ray and all the other Mossman brats kicked the bucket or mysteriously vanished, whichever came first. Yesterday, he had been sure he knew everything there was to know about House Green and a fair amount about the other houses. Now he wasn't sure.

The longer he spent around the infuriating and insufferable Yarra, the less he thought he knew. She was a violent criminal, a murderer. She deserved to be sent back to whatever hellhole they had pulled her out of, preferably the deepest, darkest pit in Trepidation, yet she was treated like family by the Mossmans – loved.

Royce had watched, completely by accident, as Ray sat on the edge of her bed with a bowl of soup in hand and pressed steaming spoonfuls to her lips. He really hadn't meant to be there – honest. He had been on his way to the roof, to the roost, where their fastest messenger birds lived to send messages to the families of the slaughtered soldiers. But . . . once he had seen Ray sitting there caring for her like one of his own, even as Kelly lay unconscious on the next bed, he had to see.

So he watched as his lord spoon-fed her the soup, fed her the whole bowl and then half a loaf of bread, held a glass of water to her lips, and glared at her until she drank it.

'How long has it been since you last ate?' the lord asked the assassin with genuine tenderness and warmth. 'How long since you've seen the sun? Since you've gone a day without being shackled?'

Royce watched as Ray stroked her filthy matted hair, a finger trailing along her jaw and her too-pale skin. The smile Yarra gave in answer was more of a grimace. Her already death-pale skin blanched further, and she lurched forward, collapsing over the side of the bed in time to empty the contents of her stomach onto the floor, everything Ray had just forced her to consume emptied in one go and now spreading across the floor.

Ray's expression was one of horrified desperation – and sadness, such deep sadness and regret. He opened his mouth but said nothing. Royce knew that words could not always convey one's feelings, felt that what Ray longed to say could not be said with mere words. Whatever these two shared, it was deeper than words could express, far deeper.

Ray just stood, crossed the room to the storage cupboard in the far corner, retrieved a mop, and proceeded to clean up. When he was done, he wiped a damp cloth over her mouth and manoeuvred her back onto the bed.

'I'll bring you more soup,' he said.

She made a small broken noise, like a moan but not.

'You'll stay here until you can keep food down,' Ray said. 'I will not let you be chained again. Not while you're so weak.'

'That's never stopped you before,' she whispered, the words barely a breath past her lips.

Ray's face was a picture of despair, of utter soul-crushing defeat. Then he was gone.

Yarra leaned back against her pillows with a sigh, eyes closed, a single pearl tear sliding down her face.

Royce waited for Ray to return, to bring with him another bowl of soup, but he never came. Instead, Zenon entered the infirmary, bearing the bowl in one hand and heavy chains in the other. The old soldier nodded respectfully to Matt as he passed by Kelly's bed and stopped at the foot of Yarra's.

For the next hour, Zenon sat with the girl, patiently feeding her mouthfuls of soup, waiting in silence as the first half was emptied in retching, hacking coughs into the bucket Zenon had placed by the bed.

The second half was consumed much slower, each spoonful followed by a grimace, a gulp of water, and another grimace – but it stayed down.

When at last, this second bowl was emptied, Zenon took a step back from the bed. It looked to Royce like pity the old soldier showed on his ancient face as he held out the chains and fastened them around the slim wrists Yarra offered obediently up.

'I'm sorry' was all Zenon said as he led her, limping and shivering, from the infirmary.

Ray's words to her clearly meant nothing. Ray had said she shouldn't be chained, had said she was to remain in bed, and now Zenon was leading her away, her wrists once again bound in heavy, magic-stifling iron chains. It was almost enough to bring a smile to his lips. For an hour, Royce had stood and watched in silence. Instead of smiling, he frowned.

Injured and still pathetically weak, she had allowed herself to be chained, allowed herself to be confined, *allowed*, because after what she had done to the werewolves, Royce was convinced that if there was something she didn't want to do, there was no force on earth that could make her do it. But she had allowed herself to be chained, even though she no doubt knew it would greatly hinder her healing process, even though she knew, as he did, that Ray hadn't wanted this. She had allowed this to happen.

Which led to the biggest question her annoying presence had raised: who exactly was she?

Who was Yarra White? Was she a true descendant of House White or a member of a long-lost branch family? What was her connection to the Mossman family, and why did they act like they both owed her everything and resented her very existence? Why was she treated like a criminal when the White family was supposedly the most powerful family in the Rainbow? What had she done to warrant such hatred? Why had she been in Trepidation? Was she really as powerful as the legends claimed?

And more importantly, what would happen when Yarra was tired of being kept prisoner and decided to take matters into her own hands? She had been chained again, locked in a guarded, warded prison cell. But what if she decided she wanted to leave? Once she recovered, what was to stop her slaughtering them all?

As mad as it made him, as infuriating as it was to put almost a century's worth of planning on hold, Royce knew he needed more information. He would not stage a coup within House Green until he was certain he would win, until he was sure that annoying and infuriating assassin girl was not going to slaughter them all. He would not risk it all until he was sure to succeed and had the knowledge to see it to completion.

She was a wild card, an unknown variable. But Royce would not let her stop him from completing his task.

He would be the most knowledgeable person to ever lead the Rainbow. He would be feared. It was entirely doable. All he would have to do would be to secret himself in the actual library for a short time. He had always been good at cramming. Perhaps he would even discover what was so important in or about all those books the Mossman brats had almost given their lives to protect.

Yes, House Green was charged with protecting knowledge, all knowledge, whether it be connected to the Rainbow or the government or history or Verstra in general. All knowledge was protected and hoarded inside the Ivy Library.

It wasn't like he was leaving the larger library unguarded either. Ray had taken control again as lord, his siblings were recovering, and his own loyal guards now flooded the halls. Should anything arise, there would be sufficient people to handle it.

Royce made one last final check on the Mossman family: Matt still as a statue on the edge of Kelly's bed; Annika viciously beating the crap out of her training dummy with a pair of twin rapiers, a snarl plastered on her face and her frilly pink skirts fanning out around her; Erryk playing chess against Ray in the hall, separating the infirmary from the room they had Yarra chained, gagged, and spelled against escape; even Yarra herself sleeping peacefully despite the chains that held her suspended from the ceiling by her arms.

Then and only then did he walk the halls with purpose, striding towards the true library wing of House Green.

His goal had been to go for the generalised history books first. The only problem was he had no clue where to find them. Perhaps it was a good thing he was revising his takeover plans, seeing as he was failing to conquer one small portion of hallways, more like a labyrinth of catacombs than isles of shelves.

Even the short journey here had seemed to take an age longer than it should have. The dark redwood door barring his way had seemed to stare ominously at his back as he pushed it open. The ages-old sign, faded from the eons it had hung there, was almost illegible but Royce knew what it said and chose to ignore it. Telling someone to 'keep out' of a place that held all the answers to anything and everything they could ever want to know would never end well. It was destined to fail.

There was no light in this place, yet the very walls seemed to crawl with life. The ground moved and shifted as he walked, and he could hear creaking from deeper inside.

'Who seeks the knowledge?' a voice whispered from the darkness.

Royce shuddered. 'Who's there?'

'We are the books, the walls, the pages. Who seeks to learn?'

'I seek the truth of ages past,' Royce said, swallowing hard. 'I, I seek to know what has happened and why things are as they are.'

'Why?'

A million reasons flashed through his mind: power, leverage, a strong foundation upon which to build his empire, to ensure that the Rainbow was strong enough to repel the forced of darkness moving to destroy them all – none of those he could tell the voice, whatever it was.

'Who are you?' he asked.

'We told you,' the voice replied, something like a laugh in its voice, 'we are the walls and the books and the pages. We know all, for we are all.'

'Curiosity,' he said at last in answer to the question.

'A bargain, we will strike then, dear stranger,' the voice said.

'What do you ask?' Royce pressed cautiously, well aware he was so far out of his depth, he didn't even know if there was a bottom. Making bargains with unknown entities was taboo. You never knew what would be asked, never knew with whom you were speaking or with what you were speaking.

'In one word,' the voice said, 'tell me what had piqued your interest, and you may have access to all the secrets you desire.'

Royce opened his mouth and then shut it. He didn't know what this disembodied voice was, didn't know if it was trustworthy, if it owed loyalty to House Green and the Mossmans, if it was a demon who had taken advantage of the downed wards to sneak into the stronghold of House

Green. Was it worth sacrificing everything on a whim of trust in this creature he couldn't see? For this . . . yes, yes it was.

'There is nothing you can say that will shock me,' the voice said, 'but do not answer, and you will find nothing but darkness within these halls.'

'Yarra,' he said. 'I am curious because of Yarra.'

Such silence filled the pitch-black halls, a still silence, almost as if the creature was so stunned, it forgot to speak.

'Yarra . . . White?' it asked, incredulous. The darkness pressed in on him like a living thing; he could feel it trace fingers across his skin. 'The legend returns after all these years?'

'So she claims, but there is no proof as to her identity, no way to know if she is a fake or a spy, and no one is saying anything.'

'Hair as dark as night with eyes as cold and grey as stone. Does that sound like the girl to you?'

'You have described her to a T,' Royce said bitterly.

'You may not like what you find, child,' the voice said, fading as if its owner was retreating.

The further away it got, the brighter the halls became. Darkness receded, revealing shelves of books, shelves upon shelves upon shelves, each with piles of books stacked high on top of them and to the sides, all the way up to the roof, making a wall of dusty old titles. Royce scowled; he was no child.

As the darkness receded into all but the farthest of shadowed corners, all Royce's previous questions seemed to pale in comparison to the one he found poised on his lips now. Faced with imminent answers to everything he could ever hope to know, he was shocked to find his hands still.

Unable to grasp the first volume he laid eyes on, a conveniently named *History of the Rainbow*, Royce stared after the darkness, doing a perfect imitation of a goldfish.

'Who are you?' he asked it and received no reply.

10

Books

How he had managed to find a complete encyclopaedia of the Rainbow without looking or trying made him pause for only a moment before Royce concluded the mysterious voice was helping him, leading him in the right direction.

He flipped through the first few pages and then through the first few chapters – nothing here he didn't know already. Royce was nothing if not through; he had done his research before attempting to take over House Green, research that had included learning about all seven houses. But his confidence had been shattered by that annoying assassin. He had more questions than answers. Better to start at the bottom, learn everything over.

Long have the members of House Red been misjudged and wrongly accused. Often the cause of inter-house disputes, family Oxblood does its duty like any other loyal to the everlasting power of the Rainbow. Blessed with the extremely powerful elemental magic of fire has ingrained into the family line a fierceness and wild war-like quality that does not suit the peaceful times the Rainbow creates. Being one of four houses to possess an elemental-based power has, throughout history, given some members of House Red an inflated sense of ego. This too has led to conflict both external and within, although, like their warrior tendencies, this has been firmly dealt with by the White and has so far caused no permanent harm to the structure and well-being of the Rainbow.

Royce squinted down at the page, the letters blurring slightly as his brows knitted together in thought. This book gave similar overviews of all the houses except the White. He would get to them eventually. There had to be one book in this vast treasure trove of paper knowledge that held some kernel of truth about that family. He would find it eventually. It was only a matter of time. But if he was going to go back to the beginning, he might as well do it in order.

Standing, Royce wandered the rows of books and volumes. Like before, the book he wanted found him, a volume dedicated solely to House Red, their family line and current living descendants. There was a family tree too, but he skipped over that.

Tragedy struck the Oxblood family multiple times through no fault of the Rainbow. Their predisposition towards conflict and violence led to more than one altercation with monsters outside of sanctioned Rainbow business. These conflicts took their toll, and the Oxblood family numbers dwindled. Presently, there is only one surviving member of the Oxblood family to carry on the bloodline of the main family. Although branch families carry the name, they have none of the power, and should this last remaining descendant pass away, it would take a miracle performed by the White themselves to revive the family.

There it was again, an arbitrary reference to the White family like they were nothing more than legend, a power above powers that could perform the miracle of miracles. Royce knew who this book referred to – the last remaining member of the Oxblood family, the traditional leaders of House Red, Ferric Oxblood and his wife, Shaniqua. All this, he knew already. It was reassuring to know that not everything he thought he knew was wrong.

Royce returned to his original book, *History of the Rainbow*, and flicked to the next chapter.

Compared to the violence of House Red, the protectors of House Orange are a placid family, calm and caring in the face of Red's anger-fuelled rage. This kindness, however, did not save them from being falsely accused of many of Red's wrongdoings. The Dijon family trait, their defining characteristic, is their fiery red eyes. This trait, much to the dismay of family Dijon, has often led them to be misidentified as members of the aforementioned house. This misidentification inadvertently bought the families together, families Oxblood and Dijon historically collaborating to wreak vengeance on the monsters greater than the two could achieve apart. Family Dijon possesses the rare and extremely powerful healing ability, a power the Rainbow has utilised more than once to save House Red and many members of other houses from serious injury.

Royce did not need to go and find a book dedicated to House Orange. He knew what had happened to them. Their kindness became a weakness. Their compassion allowed them to be tamed, corralled into an area of powerlessness, coerced into situations they had no chance of surviving, leaving only one, Izrabella, a young girl about the same age as Annika Mossman, a sweet little thing, too pure for words. It was almost a shame Alexander and Theresa Sheresta had stolen power from her and were carefully orchestrating her death to appear natural and tragic. The loss of her healing ability would be a blow for sure, but they would survive. The Rainbow always survived.

The most whimsical of the seven families comprising the Rainbow remains so even to this day, always fond of filling their halls with laughter and joy. It has become tradition for House Yellow to be ruled by a large family, often ruling long into their lives, lordship of House Yellow rarely changes hands; thus, their power remains stable. This stability contrasts with the elemental power family Goldenrod has over air. Branch families and the main family often live together, interact, and mingle; as such, their power is passed more easily between them. This widespread of power can cause confusion when attempting to discern the identity of a branch family member from a member of the main family; fortunately, such confusion can be nullified easily. All Goldenrod family members with true heritage to their ancestors possess burning eyes of gold.

This time, he did not even have to move around for the book to present itself: the volume chronicling the lives and times of the Goldenrod family – who the current lord was, who their family was, when they passed, and who inherited. It even spoke of branch families, their downfalls and triumphs. No other house showed such care or consideration for distant cousins, not even the Mossmans.

Following the death of her beloved father and benevolent ruler of House Yellow, Charlotte Goldenrod has been elevated to lord of House Yellow. With her lover and soon-to-be-wedded husband, Charles, she has borne two children. Harriet and James, who, at this moment, represent the next generation of aptly named airheaded rulers, although the Goldenrod tendency to have large families' future children is almost a given. The Goldenrod family future and, as such, the future of House Yellow looks to remain as stable as it has in years past and well into the future.

Royce almost slammed the book in frustration. He turned back to *History of the Rainbow*, skipped completely over the section about House Green and the Mossman family. He knew enough about them; he lived with them. What was written inside one book could not convey more than what he had learned these past decades. He moved straight on to House Blue and the Beryl family.

Rounding up the four houses blessed with elemental power is House Blue, led by family Beryl. Houses Red and Blue, thanks mostly in part to their polar-opposite elemental powers, have been historically at odds. The famous tempers of House Red can be matched only by the tempers of the Beryl family in House Blue. Their tempestuous nature can either soothe or destroy, often in equal part, as is the nature of their element history, which has shown that House Blue cycles through periods of peace and disarray.

The book on the Beryl family presented itself, but Royce didn't open it. He was in close contact with Lynda and Dean Couvrette, the family who had disposed of the last remaining Beryls, Meredith and Taiga. Royce modelled his own takeover after the successful overthrow the Couvrettes had staged. Both Meredith and Taiga Beryl were powerful in their own right; both had pull with the other houses, possessed the elemental power of House Blue, yet Lynda and Dean had toppled them. It was a feat Royce hoped to replicate in House Green, a feat he would replicate.

Perhaps the most misunderstood of all the great houses of the Rainbow is, without a doubt, the Aster family of House Indigo. Often called eccentric and scorned by the other houses and monsters alike, the Aster family specialises in poisons and toxins. Their skill is often the difference between life and death in times of war. Their highly valuable and life-saving skill has not gone unnoticed by the Rainbow, often receiving praise from the other houses. Their steep success rates are often undermined by the efforts of the individual. Quirkiness and emotional detachments that rival those of the White have led to the steady decrease in Aster family numbers.

As far as Royce knew, there hadn't been an Aster leading House Indigo for over one hundred years. He reached for the book on them purely to find out if any of them still lived, if there was any chance of their descendants rising up to reclaim their birthright, also to see if there was any further mention of the White. He had never heard of them being mentally challenged, but after meeting Yarra, he could see that might have had a basis in fact. Yarra was at best eccentric, at worst deranged and certifiably insane, not a combination he relished in anyone, certainly not an assassin, especially one housed within House Green.

The installation of Joseph Moon as leader of House Indigo was well received by the lords of the other houses. Many were relieved to have the reins of such an important house handed over to someone who was not likely to burn the place down or accidentally poison the entirety of the Rainbow. Since that time, House Indigo had been run by the extremely capable Mr Moon and his growing family. The Asters have not died out, however. Being relieved from the duty of rule seems to have allowed the Asters to expand their fields of testing. Their powers remain an asset to the Rainbow, and although young Davinder and Katya are untested, the Rainbow maintains high hopes for their success in the future.

So there were two Asters left alive, children by the sound of it, or they had been children when the book was being written. No further mention of House White, and from the remaining number of pages in the book, it appeared House White definitely did not have its own chapter. The mysterious voice had piled up books around him, books about House Red and House Blue but no books about House White, no books whose title suggested they contained anything useful in his search for answers about Yarra. He had one more house left to refresh his knowledge on; then he could tackle the problem of Yarra's missing family information.

The title of most misunderstood belongs squarely to House Indigo, but House Violet comes in a close second. House Violet also lays claim to the title of most untrustworthy, most feared, and most unfortunate, largely feared and hated by all those outside the Rainbow and some members within. It is no surprise the Amaryllis family was ostracised and hunted. Revered as the Rainbow's best spies and unrivalled infiltrators, the Amaryllis's power over shadows and darkness is highly sought after and feared. Contrary to their power and the secretive skill set that made them feared across all nations, many of the Amaryllis family have large, outgoing personalities. Historically, the members of family Amaryllis have possessed red hair, making marking their appearance an easy task. This has had an adverse effect on the safety of the family and strength of House Violet. Enemies far and wide attacked and slaughtered those possessing the Amaryllis red-haired gene. This indiscriminate killing continued until the Amaryllis family existed almost entirely in shadow, and House Violet was turned over to the control of Kayneth Kor.

Well, that explained why Kayneth was so assuredly leader of House Violet. At the bottom of the page in big red sad letters was a short sentence declaring the fate of family Amaryllis: No Living Family Members.

There. the book ended. Royce closed *History of the Rainbow* and sighed into the silence. Nothing on the White. Nothing about their fabled power. He'd have to look harder elsewhere. If finding out the truth were easy, he would have done it sooner or not bothered at all.

11

Answers

Yarra hummed softly to herself. Hanging from her wrists, suspended in mid-air by iron chains, her latest wounds not yet healed, she hummed. There was precious little else to do in her latest prison cell.

As prison cells went, this one was almost nice. Unlike other cells she had been in, this one had a window, although there were bars across the glass. It was nice to have the sun fall on her face, even if the light irritated her skin and the scratches that marred it. How long had it been since she'd seen the sun? Thirty years? Forty? Probably closer to the fifty years she had been in Trepidation. Now she was out, free.

What did the Rainbow want with her? Why had they finally made a move? And not just any move but a move that rocked the very foundations of Verstran society. According to Verstra law, any criminal sentenced to the Halls of Trepidation was never to be released. It was a death camp. Few had ever escaped. Those who had gotten out quickly vanished. Why had the Rainbow staged such a dangerous rescue mission? Why, when it was their decree that had landed her there in the first place?

She had sources far and wide, all of them monsters in their own right, fellow assassins and thieves as numerous as the vampires and ghouls she befriended, many of whom had ways of communicating with the world outside the halls and of getting messages in. If something had happened, she would have known.

Unless something really, truly bad had happened, bad enough to silence all her ears and blind all the eyes loyal only to her. Something that

52

bad would certainly warrant a move as large as the one the Rainbow had just pulled.

Yarra rotated her wrists slowly, skin grating against the iron, her magic repulsed by its touch. She tucked her legs up to her chest, clicked her fingers, and dropped like a stone.

By the time she landed, she was already rolling, throwing herself over her shoulder over and over until all momentum was exhausted and she came to a stop. She exited the final roll by standing smoothly and stretched her arms above her head.

'Ahhh, right then. Where to start . . .'

She glanced guiltily at the door, towards the guards most likely posted outside, tasked with keeping her in. Too bad for them. She was leaving – now.

Unless . . .

'Help!' she called, knocking on the door, pleading pathetically. 'Help!'

'You don't need help, girlie,' came the calm reply.

Yarra glared at the door. Of course, it was him. Who else? 'You may be right, Zenon, but it would be helpful.'

Her cell door swung open to reveal Ray's former captain of the guard. The ancient but mercilessly kind man smiled down at her. She was pulled into a hug before she could do anything to stop it. With the hug came the warm embrace of his magic, magic that sought out her many injuries and soothed them, urged them to close and heal.

'It's good to see you again, girlie,' he said softly.

'What's going on, Zenon?' she asked. 'What has happened? Why was I freed?'

Only with Zenon could Rule One be broken.

'Things are bad, girlie. Real bad. You heard what happened to House Blue?'

Yarra shook her head.

'It was not long after your trial.'

Yarra hissed at the memory.

'It's all right, girlie, I don't blame you. Neither did House Blue. Aye, they may have voted to exile you with the rest of them, but after you left, they put up a hell of a fight in your defence.'

'What happened?'

'Kayneth Kor,' Zenon spat. 'You remember him, right? Nasty man, head of House Violet. Kicked up a storm, he did. Backed fully by Indigo and Orange. Ray spoke up for you too, but Clyde was firm, unmoving. Kayneth was ruthless. Spouting all sorts of lies about you and about the Beryls. Insinuated they were in league with you, monster sympathisers.'

Clyde Mossman, Ray's father, had always been steadfast in his ways. Once his mind had been made up about anything, there was no way in hell to change it.

'They were replaced,' Yarra said, voice flat.

Zenon nodded. Yarra swore – colourfully.

'Ray said I hadn't been bound. I thought that was odd. I should have asked him why. I should have made him tell me. No, I should have known. I saw that the deck was not full, that our hand had been cut.'

'You were needed here,' Zenon said. 'You saved Kelly's life and Matt's.'

Yarra shook her head. 'To bind me, the Rainbow needs cooperation from at least four original family members. That binding was cut when I was exiled. Only three came to get me from Trepidation. I should have known something had happened to the Beryls when House Blue didn't show. I did know. I think I must have known. But I was free. After so, so many years, I was free. Only to trapped and caged again, bound again, always in chains, always caged. Always.'

'That's not all that's happened since you left, girlie. There is talk of a war. Of uncontrolled fighting and slaughter. Countless deaths are expected on both sides.'

'And that's why they pulled me out? Because of the pledge?'

The pledge was a closely guarded secret. Only two people outside members of the original families knew about it in any capacity. Zenon was one.

'The pledge may have been the driving factor for Ray and Houses Red and Yellow, but they got you out under a different guise – advisor and fighter. You will be expected to fight with our armies, girlie. Whether you want to or not. To that end, you would have been safer in the halls.'

Her status as Verstra's best assassin guaranteed she was a skilled fighter. Not everyone wanted to be killed. Most put up a fight; some were experts in their own right. To have killed them practically assured her combative prowess.

Her higher-profile kills included a vampire ancient, a vampire so old, entire covens and hierarchies were created by vampires they'd turned, and a wraith queen. The Wraith were like bees in the sense that they protected their queen to the last; without their queen, the wraith had no direction, no purpose.

And those were just her monster kills. There were others too – many others.

Yarra hung her head. Oh, this was just great. 'I have heard nothing. About any of this. My sources have been quiet. More than quiet – they have been silent. There has been no sign of this. Not even whispers.'

'Is that unusual?' he asked her.

'Very.' She looked at him full in the face, slate-grey eyes shining. 'I need to go. Now. Find my sources, root out what is really going on. Blind those who need no longer see, listen hard to those who have the right thing to say.'

'I will stall them as long as I can, girlie, but Ray will want to brief you on the war, on your role as advisor. There may not be time to seek out long-lost sources just yet. And Royce will be keeping an eye on you. He's ordered all the guards to kill you if you even so much as attempt to leave. Besides' – Zenon smiled slightly, just a slight twitching of his lips, but it was there – 'you're still hurt, and Ray won't let you leave until all the soup in this place is gone.'

Yarra frowned and then grinned at him, showing all her teeth, and strode from her cell, easy as pie. Zenon closed the cell door behind her and stood to attention again as if she were still inside. An assassin such as she did not pass up any chance to explore and add to the vast arsenal that made Rule One so formidable.

Ray may have needed to bind her to keep her here, but his magic was powerful enough to alert him if she did indeed try to leave. He might even have enough power to stop her – for a time.

She could hunt her eyes and ears later. There were other ways to get to the bottom of this, to find out if this war was real, if slaughter was really going to break out over Verstra once more.

12

Mystery

Having found nothing in the books and not wanting to ask his mysterious, all-knowing disembodied friend, Royce decided to channel the deceased Amaryllis family and took to spying. Lurking in the shadows, he followed the Mossmans, watching them, listening, hoping to learn anything about Yarra and her family, anything that could take him closer to the truth.

His first kernel of information came from Annika. His favourite Mossman brat was her usual charming self, meaning that she was angry and bitter and muttering murderous plans for the destruction of all monster kind and sometimes even the brutal murder of her elder brother, with whom she was currently arguing. It was the main reason he liked her so much more than her siblings: she disliked Ray almost as much as he did.

'Why is she locked up?' Annika demanded.

Ray sighed heavily. 'Because she is a criminal, Annika. To the soldiers, she is a criminal. A criminal. She was in the Halls of Trepidation. Do you know what that means?'

'Of course I know what that means!' she snapped.

'Really? OK, then enlighten me. Well? *Well?* Tell me, Annika. Tell me what it means.'

Royce could see Annika bite her lip, her mahogany hair newly washed and twirled into pigtails once again, changing her image from one of burning anger and humiliation to one of comedy. Her emerald eyes burned, glinting like embers in the lamplight of the training room.

The place had become a sanctuary to Annika in the aftermath of the werewolves' attack on the library. She had hardly left its walls, preferring to hone her sword skills than to eat at the dinner table, and would rather sharpen her knife-throwing skills than sit at Kelly's bedside and worry over her recovery, slow as it was.

The room itself was not unpleasant. It was wide and open, located in the far corner of the library with windows on two sides, letting in early-morning light but falling into darkness in the evening; it was, in fact, quite a nice room. Its elegance was not marred by the decapitated mannequins littering the floors or massacred targets pinned to the walls, nor was the sheer number of weapons available in the cupboards or shelved on the walls a sight that drew negative attention from the overall elegance of the room.

Perhaps the only downside was the presence of the two people currently occupying the room. Annika, dressed in a soft pink gown cinched at the waist and drenched in sweat from her workout, clutched a sword in each hand and glared at her brother. Ray had discarded his green cloak in favour of more comfortable pants and shirt in varying shades of brown and white. His arms were folded; his face, if not his tone, was neutral.

'She only went to Trepidation to get away from you lords,' Annika said with no small amount of satisfaction in her voice. 'You should let her go.'

'I can't let her go. The men fear her. They see her as a criminal because to them, she is one. Even if I know it to be a lie. Even if I know she would do nothing to harm anyone within these walls.'

'How did she survive the poison?' Annika asked softly. 'How did you know she wasn't dead?'

'Poison is part of her nature,' Ray said with a slight tilt of his lips. 'It takes time for her body to work through it, but in the end, it's all the same with her.'

'How do you know?' Annika squinted up at her brother suspiciously. 'The pledge would have had to be broken for you to find that out. How come Father didn't have your head?'

'It was Father's fault.' Ray's face became vacant as he remembered. 'Father was tasked with tracking her down after she escaped. He tracked her to the heart of the Ghost Lands, where the marshes meet the Forgotten Lands.'

Annika frowned. 'And she was poisoned?'

Ray nodded. 'The fog of the Forgotten Lands is toxic. Yarra fled there, unknowing, and Father followed. He retrieved her only after the poison had knocked her out. She was still breathing but for weeks after the Rainbow lived in fear of her death.'

'But she woke up,' Annika finished. 'She was fine.'

'After a time,' Ray said. 'It was about three weeks, I think, before she woke up. Her parents wanted Father to die for failing to uphold the pledge. But as she lived, there was nothing they could do.'

Annika let out a long sigh, relief colouring her voice. 'So there really was nothing to worry about after all.'

'She could still have died,' Ray said. 'Trepidation has left her weaker than I've ever seen her before. Weaker than even she believes is possible.'

'That's no reason to lock her up.'

'the guards don't know her like we do. They don't know about the pledge. They only see her as a criminal. They only see what she has done.'

Annika sneered, 'You have to let her go.'

Ray shook his head. 'I can't. The guards would riot. Have you forgotten what she did?'

'I don't remember it,' Annika snapped. 'How could I remember it? I wasn't born yet, but I remember the stories. I remember Ma telling what she did. I remember the stories Ma told me about the White, about their power and importance, and the pledge. She made me repeat it to her every night. Every word over and over until it was second nature, as easy as breathing. Yarra is nothing like the stories Ma told. Yarra was kind, *is* kind, and she is not a criminal.'

'Father did what he must. The other lords did what they had to do!'

'They banished her!' Annika screamed. 'The last of House White, the sole survivor of her family!'

'They had no choice!' Ray yelled back. 'The pledge prevented them from carrying out the death sentence she rightfully earned. They had to do something!'

'She is not a criminal!' Annika said again.

'She may have not been then, but since she fled, she has done many unforgivable things. She joined a militia, for gods' sake. A militia, Annika. Don't you see? Even if she wasn't before, she is now.'

'So she joined a militia,' Annika said. 'So what?'

Ray pressed two fingers to the bridge of his nose, breathed deeply. 'Remember the attack on Norvus? The battle between House Blue's forces and the rebel army?'

Annika nodded. It was one of the most famous battles of recent times. Annika had studied it intensely in her history lessons. Despite the battle having taken place almost a century ago, she knew it inside and out.

'Yarra's militia made up a large part of the rebel army. For our safety and her own, she will remain locked up until the Rainbow deems it necessary for her to act.'

Annika balled her fists around the hilts of her swords. 'You have to let her go.'

'No,' Ray said, turning on his heel, and strode away. 'I'm sorry.'

Annika screamed, a sound of pure earth-shattering rage. She spun and hurled her swords into the nearest dummy, splitting it open from head to toe, and then glared at her brother's retreating back.

'*I hate you!*'

Ray paused. He showed no sign of Annika's words hurting him, but they had to have struck a nerve. 'She's probably already escaped, you know,' he said softly. 'She's probably already escaped and wandering the library, an assassin free within our walls.'

'What will you do?' Annika sounded almost scared.

Ray shrugged, not turning around. 'Nothing. I told Erryk to wait in the war room and to brief her when she shows up.'

Royce was sure his jaw clanged off the floor. The echoes still haunting his ears, he took a step forward – and then another and then another and then another – until he was well into the training room, facing the two Mossmans with a stunned expression of pure, befuddled shock plastered over his face.

'She cannot be allowed to know anything about this war,' he said, short, sharp, right to the point, even if his tone was perhaps slightly disrespectful.

'She was pulled from Trepidation to be our advisor,' Ray said tersely. 'I will not send her back simply because you do not trust her.'

'What about when the bodies start dropping?' he asked. 'What then? Will you send her back to Trepidation then?'

Ray shifted from foot to foot, clearly uncomfortable and unwilling to so much as glance at Annika. 'If that happens, then she will be sent back. She will be sent back in chains. But that will not happen. Yarra is here to advise, and here, she will stay.'

Royce hung his head, teeth digging deep into his lip. 'She is an assassin,' he ground out, 'a criminal. She knows nothing of infantry warfare to how to fight as part of a team. To include her in strategy talks is ludicrous. Worse even. It will mean the deaths of countless soldiers.'

'She's not a criminal!' Annika snapped viciously.

'Feel free to train her if you feel her skills are insufficient,' Ray said, shrugging and striding from the training room. 'She should be in the war room by now,' he called over his shoulder.

Royce wasted a moment staring after him in abject horror. The extent to which this lord devalued the lives of his soldiers was so astounding, so shocking, Royce's brain refused to process it. Once his brain had caught up with the shock, he turned a despairing look to Annika. His favourite Mossman sneered at him, her expression one that suggested she knew her brother was being unreasonable but that she also knew there was nothing she could do to stop him.

With a muttered curse, Royce headed towards the war room. He was more determined than ever to bring down Ray Mossman. No longer was this vendetta for himself. He now planned revolution to save them all. When he was in charge, criminals would stay in whatever rotting hellhole they found themselves thrown into.

They would not be bought in as consultants, even if they were world-famous assassins who had proved themselves to be significantly skilled – and somehow immune to poisons.

Member of the mysterious White or not, criminals should remain in their prisons. He had to find something in her past that could scare her into submission. There had to be something in a past as shadowed as hers that she feared the world knowing.

He would train her, as Ray had suggested. He would put her through hell, beat her down at every opportunity, break her – mind, body, and spirit – and then serve her with whatever deep, dark secrets he had uncovered and leash her to him. He may firmly believe she deserved to spend the rest of her immortal life rotting in the halls of Trepidation, but he was not stupid enough to pass up such a golden opportunity.

By the end of this, he would have Verstra's most famous and deadly assassin firmly under his thumb – his pawn, to use as he will.

13

Traitor

Now, of course, all he had to do was find her.

Royce found Erryk in the war room, standing over a large map showing the whole of Verstra. The boundaries between the lands owned by each of the houses and the Wild Lands, dominated by the monsters of the world, were red. The buildings that held significance either to the Rainbow or to the wider Verstran world, such as the Ivy Library, headquarters of House Green, were marked on the map in blue.

Further markers in green and black detailed the known movements of the monster armies. Erryk was moving them around like chess pieces, positioning them on the Amaranth Ruins, where House Red operated, and then on the Cerulean Gardens near House Blue. The young Mossman did not look up as Royce entered.

'You just missed her,' Erryk said, holding out a small crumpled piece of paper, still without looking up from his work.

Scowling, Royce took the paper and scanned the line of wobbling text, like the person who had written it was having trouble controlling her hands, like they were weakened from constant shackling and fifty years locked underground in the worst prison Verstra had to offer – or she was laughing.

Casting eyes skyward often leads to blindness.

'She's insane,' Royce muttered, staring aghast at the paper.
'Huh?' Erryk asked, clearly not listening. 'Yes, I suppose so.'

'What does this mean?'

'Put simply, she's taunting you.' Erryk carefully placed the pieces back on the map and, resting his chin on folded fingers, finally raised emerald eyes to Royce. 'She is saying, "Come and get me," or, if you rather, "Catch me if you can". No doubt she knows you want to train her, although I can't fathom why, and wants to remind you that she is the best.'

Royce snorted. 'The best? So? Where is she?'

The Mossman brat merely shrugged and pointed wildly to the left. Royce almost snorted, snarled — almost. He hurried from the room, fuming. Where could she have gone? Where in this whole entire, very vast library could she have gone?

'Zenon!' he snapped, swinging by the room where the girl should by all rights still be chained. 'With me.'

The old soldier hurried to keep pace. Zenon was perhaps Royce's greatest achievement. Zenon had been captain of the guard before him, a loyal and long-serving devotee of House Green and the lords Mossman — yet Royce had replaced him as captain and then turned the old soldier to his side, convinced him to turn on his long-time friends.

'Report!' he barked out. 'Tell me what you know of Yarra White.'

'She is not as she was,' Zenon said, huffing slightly. 'When last I saw her, it was more than seventy-five years ago. She was very different then. Trepidation changed her.'

'How so?'

'she is harsher now than she ever was. Thinner too. She has lost weight she could not afford to lose — and no doubt muscle with it.'

'In your opinion, would you think it wise to include her in this war?'

Royce held his breath as the old soldier pursed his lips in thought. This was not simply reporting on Lord Ray's thoughts; this was betraying an old friend and throwing her under the bus — literally.

'Aye, in the past, she would have been a valuable asset. But now . . .' Zenon shook his head. 'She is changed.'

Royce waited for a spell, for Zenon to pull himself together. The old soldier was still shaking his head, sadness etched across his features.

'Where would she go?' Royce asked gently. 'The girl you knew, where would she go?'

Perhaps to understand the girl now, he needed to understand who she was and how Trepidation changed her.

'Try the infirmary,' Zenon said walking away, his head bowed. 'There is only one family she's ever cared for. I doubt even Trepidation could change that. And if it has . . . well then, God help us all.'

That was interesting . . . What could he mean by that?

Royce hid a small smile and decided it was wise to pursue other options as well as pose delicate questions to one or more of the Mossmans. If Annika could be convinced to give over information on Yarra, she might prove to be his one single best source of information. If not, well, then these training sessions might prove to be just as fruitful.

He already had more questions. But now, faced with a possible goldmine of answers, he was decidedly more optimistic about his whole situation.

At least until he strode into the infirmary with completely innocent intentions of checking up on Kelly Mossman – well, that was what he would have told anyone who asked him – and saw Yarra free from her chains, in near-perfect health. She was helping Kelly sit and then stand up and test the fragile healing of her wounds.

'You can do so much,' Kelly said weakly. 'Why do you choose to suffer?'

'it is not the weak who choose to suffer but the strong,' Yarra answered. 'It is the strong who know suffering and live regardless of the pain they know it will cause.'

Kelly gave her a look, which, although filled with pain, conveyed enough of her thoughts for Yarra to smile.

'I mean' – Kelly winced – 'why didn't you heal yourself before now?'

'Do you want revenge, Kelly? For what they did to you?' Yarra asked in a surprisingly soft voice. 'Because revenge is for madmen and fools, and as you are neither, it would be a waste of your time.'

Kelly laughed or tried to before her pain doubled her over and had her hissing through her teeth to keep from crying out.

Yarra was instantly by her side, holding her arm, clutching her like a baby. Then her skin began to glow; a soft, almost silver glow formed around her body, flowing from her into Kelly. The Mossman brat's winces lessened and then faded, and Royce could see her wounds visibly heal.

The puckered edge of that slash on her face smoothed, the tatters of skin clinging to her left arm knitted more firmly together as Yarra healed her.

Royce could see Yarra's wounds too were sealing. The deep gouges in her arms and legs were evening out. No longer were they deep enough to cut bone now; they were mere pale bands of skin against her already-pale flesh. It seemed she could not heal others without also healing herself.

'So you waited to heal me because you wanted me to give up on revenge?' Kelly asked, laughing for real this time. 'Why?'

'Revenge is for madmen and fools,' Yarra repeated, 'and as you are neither, it would be a waste of your time.'

Royce snuck out of the infirmary, frowning. How could Yarra have the power to heal others? According to the book, that was the power of House Orange. Add that to what he had seen before when she had slipped from her bonds like a shadow, bonds that were supposedly magic proof, and rushed to the library to promptly slaughter countless werewolves, utilising the magic of shadows that was the domain of House Violet. Ray had said something about her nature being poison too; poisons were House Indigo's speciality. She had manifested and demonstrated the powers of three Houses. Could she do more? And where did her seer power come from? Again, he was left with more questions than answers.

Was it possible that she could have more than one power? From what the book had said on the powers of House Violet and the Amaryllis family, he knew that the ability to turn to shadows was an ability they had possessed, but that didn't explain why Yarra could do it. It didn't make sense.

As angry as he was to see that Yarra had somehow escaped her chains, he had come to the realisation that chains were useless against her. As long as she was willing to sit still and wait, chains served no more purpose than decoration. He'd have to devise some other way of dealing with her. Perhaps whatever information he uncovered about her and her family could give him leverage. Royce had no qualms blackmailing the girl into submission, none at all.

Of course, the simplest course of action would have been to ask Yarra directly, but there was something about the way she talked. The riddles within which she seemed to revel were unnerving, to say the least. And he didn't want to seem obvious. He would look like a fool if he outright asked Yarra about her family history. He would assign Zenon to train her. The old soldier might have more of a chance prying information from her.

He would find his answers elsewhere. Annika would have to do.

14

Training

Yarra knew there was a time and a place for confrontation. When she still could not keep down a single bowl of soup was probably not that time. But she was an assassin, and all her fights happened in the dark, at a time and place of her choosing. Subterfuge was her game. There was a time and a place for that too.

Her meeting with Erryk had gone horribly. Rule One had been slashed. How was she supposed to be the smartest person in the room when the only other person was a genius-level strategist who had had the past fifty years to learn the little nuances of this coming war she knew nothing about? She only had her outdated knowledge and a small army of eyes and ears that were both deaf and blind.

She had suggested seeking out Nerys, her long-time friend and high commander of the werewolf government, the queen of the northern reaches in the werewolf council of twelve. But Erryk had shut that down in an instant. The werewolves had attacked them, after all, and couldn't be trusted.

She had then suggested venturing into the Ghost Lands to talk with the ghosts there, many of whom were loyal to the Rainbow; several were loyal only to her. But Erryk had shut that down as well.

Next, Yarra mentioned consulting Siliba. Whenever there was death, the banshees were always the first on scene. Nothing happened without them knowing, but again, Erryk shut her down.

Finally, in a near act of desperation, she asked about Achilles. This time, Erryk said nothing. But his silence was answer enough. No one had heard from her oldest friend. He had disappeared without a trace.

So she had smiled and said something about the ways of the universe crossing at the most unlikely times and geared up to have a wonderful time with Royce, wonderful because it was almost certainly a bad idea. Royce was an unknown variable, something she hadn't encountered before, a person who hated her not because of what she'd done but because of who she was – or more accurately, who she wasn't, someone who hated her because, for once, they knew nothing about her.

'Royce has expressed concerns concerning your abilities,' Ray told her. 'I have given him leave to train you. To see for himself if you are up to scratch.'

The undercurrent of 'please don't kill him' was not lost on Yarra, but she chose to pretend she hadn't heard it. *More fun that way.* She was an assassin, after all. Accidents happened. More fun in the sense that it gave her instant deniability, should something actually happen to the good captain.

Not that anything would happen. She had spent a well-documented fifty years inside Verstra's worst prison, spent a good portion of that time chained and immobile. Her muscles had deteriorated. No matter how careful she had been, how much she chose to deny it, it was true.

That fight with the werewolves should not have gone the way it had. Yes, she had won, but it had not been as quick or as painless as a similar fight would have been in the years before she was exiled. Maybe she did need this training with Royce, not that she'd ever openly admit it to anyone – ever.

When had Zenon been replaced as captain of the guard anyway? Why had he been replaced?

Why was it that House Green seemed to be hell bent on destroying Rule One?

'I'm told you don't see things the way Ray or I do. Like a dog barking at the master who feeds him,' she said, strolling casually into one of the rooms dominated by House Green's guards. She had taken care to cuff and chain herself but loosely, so the chains clanged, and she could twirl them around herself like ribbons if she chose.

She wanted to appear the meek and crippled criminal they believed her to be, let them think she was hiding her true power, let them think her the swaggering assassin that was thrown into Trepidation all those years ago, let them believe she could kill them with a look or a thought.

That, in a sense, was Rule Three: never let them see the truth. Or as she liked to think of it: fake it till you make it.

'I think I'm beginning to understand how you think,' Royce said, turning around to face her, his initial surprise hidden swiftly under a mask of contempt. She had found him, not the other way around.

'I doubt that very much,' she countered. 'I don't believe you have belief in much of anything. Or the brain power to fathom exactly how stupid you are.'

'Lord Mossman gave me the impression that you had escaped.'

Royce waved the other soldiers out of the room. They filed past Yarra, glaring and muttering. Had the daggers shot from their eyes been real, Yarra would have been dead several times over. *Shame.*

'You yourself gave me the impression you were free from chains and in hiding.'

Yarra cocked her head, 'Whatever gave you that idea? A little bird perhaps, chirping some sweet tune?'

Royce scowled at her, ground his teeth. 'I may not believe you have what it takes to advise us in this war, but Ray does. I also do not believe you have what it takes to fight alongside us. A criminal like you has no sense of duty. No sense of comradery. You would see us killed on the battlefield.'

Yarra chose to stay silent. To overlook the insults not to her but to Ray.

'But as I said, Ray disagrees. He has given me leave to train you. To educate you in the ways of infantry combat and tactics.'

'And if I refuse? Which I do, by the way. Categorically.'

'Then I will chain you to me, and I will drag you through these halls like the murderous monster that you are.'

Stone-cold eyes sparkled. 'The Rainbow is sworn to destroy all monsters. Whatever will you do? Kill me?'

Another scowl, more teeth grinding, 'There is more than one way to slay a monster.' He looked her up and down, leering a moment at her chest and waist. 'I'm going to assume those chains are for show and that you are, in fact, free. I'm also going to assume that you're trying to make some kind of point. All I can say is this – I hope you're as good as you think you are.'

Yarra's answering grin was nothing short of wicked.

'Unfortunately, I am much too busy to train you myself. Count yourself lucky. You'll be training with Zenon instead.'

With that, he promptly left, just turned on his heel and stalked out of the room, holding the door open and murmuring something to Zenon before the old soldier stepped forward and the door clanged shut behind him.

'Sorry 'bout this, girlie,' Zenon said, 'but boss's orders.'

Yarra shrugged. 'What's done is done. Our time set firmly in immovable stone. The future does not change simply because I wish it to.'

Zenon shook his head with a smile. But it was tight, strained. His eyes flicked from her face to the door Royce had closed behind him, a warning that they were not alone.

Yarra instantly understood. Her answering grin was nothing short of fiendish, mischief dancing across her face and waltzing behind suddenly burning eyes.

Yarra rushed forward, throwing her arms around the old soldier's neck before he had time to react. She made her voice sound light and carefree, childish and concerned but laced with layers of history, an old and dear friend checking in on the health of a loved one she hadn't seen in seventy-five years.

'Zenon, it's soooo good to seeee you. How have you been? Did you miss me? *Did you miss me?*'

Zenon stood there, ramrod straight. He didn't hug her back, didn't speak or even whisper well wishes of his own. Yarra pouted, a frown creasing her brow.

'How long has the cuckoo ruled the nest?' she asked quietly.

Slowly, Zenon eased his arms around her too-slight frame. 'I've missed you too, girlie,' he breathed, bringing his face close to hers. 'The cuckoo does what it will to survive. It does not matter when it came, only that it is here now, and in this nest, the cuckoo is king.'

Yarra pulled away and sketched a mock bow. 'Where shall we begin then, my liege?'

Zenon crossed his arms, smirking. 'You are to run five times around this room.'

The ensuing shouting match was so loud and so shockingly vulgar, even the carrier birds on the roof raised a cacophony in a failed attempted to drown out the noise – all for naught.

Verstra's best and most unpredictable assassin snarled softly and began her first lap around the room. The pace she set was by no means fast, scarcely faster than a brisk walk, but by the second lap, she was winded and wheezing.

They both felt it the moment Royce lost interest and moved away, the imposing presence the captain of the guard relied on to keep his underlings in line hidden but not completely suppressed as Royce watched them from the behind the door. If he had learnt anything was unclear. Whatever he had hoped to learn from seeing them together had either been confirmed or denied.

'Are you reporting to him or Ray?' she asked in a voice she rarely used, a voice reserved for when she was completely serious, a voice devoid of mischief or haughty arrogance.

'Him,' Zenon said.

'Things have changed, haven't they?'

'Aye, girlie. That, they have.' The old soldier gave her a strange look. 'Things have changed, but one thing remains. One thing hasn't and will not change for as long as I live.'

'What?' Yarra asked, hands braced on her knees, her chest heaving.

'My loyalty has always been to House Green, and it always will be.' He clapped his hands with sudden and unexpected force and barked, 'Back to running!'

Yarra completed all five laps, although she collapsed and threw up at the end of it. Zenon watched this with an impassive stare, but Yarra knew what he wanted to say.

'Tomorrow you'll run around the building,' he said. Then 'It's a miracle those werewolves didn't kill you'.

Yarra just lay there, heaving. Then she picked herself up and stumbled out of the room, passing scowling soldiers without batting an eye.

She swung by Ray's study, not really expecting to see him, grabbed the first blank page she could see, and scribbled a quick list: names of her sources, their last known locations. She finally admitted that she was in no shape to track them down herself, but someone had to do it. So far, there were only whispers of the war, musing of an army. Her sources would know the truth, one way or another. Wincing at her own weakness and cursing the memories that came unbidden to the surface and the tears those memories brought, she continued her stumbling, looking for Erryk.

15

Revelation

Royce knew Zenon would work the girl to the ground and then report to him about it, knew that unless Zenon was somehow won over by her 'charm', there was no way he was going to hear favourable things about her from him. It was clear they had been close in the past. Hopefully, that meant she would reveal things to Zenon she wouldn't to anyone else. Then Zenon would tell him. It was second-hand information at best, personal opinion at worst, but it was better than nothing.

It was beyond infuriating. His best source of information should have been the library and the disembodied voice housed amongst the books. But the voice remained silent. It gave him no information on the girl other than to sneer at the very mention of the girl's name. So he worked on how to broach the subject with Annika.

The youngest Mossman was still beating up the training dummies when Royce strode into the training room days after Zenon first beat the criminal girl to a pulp. Her movements were slowed, sluggish, like she regretted slaughtering the dummies – or crying, as it turned out.

Silent tears slipped from her eyes and rolled down her face, smearing smooth tracks across her skin. Royce stopped in his tracks, questions dying on his lips. He had always liked Annika over her siblings, but he didn't like her personally. He didn't think he knew how to comfort someone, let alone someone he didn't like. Yet here she was, a young girl crying before him.

'Are you OK?' he asked lamely.

She spun, swords instantly ready. Such rage in the glare she levelled his way.

'What do you want?' she snapped, wiping fiercely at her eyes.

'Kelly is awake,' he said lamely, grasping at the first thought that popped into his mind. Annika probably already knew this – it had happened days ago – but it was the best he could do. 'Yarra healed her.'

Swords clattered to the ground. 'Oh thank god!' Annika's hands trembled as she pressed them to her cheeks, fresh tears spilling down her face. 'She healed her,' Annika sobbed. 'She healed her . . . but how? Ray had her chained.'

Was this an act, a ruse to get him to believe that the Mossmans did not always tell one another everything, did not have the same unwavering and unshakeable trust and faith that annoying Yarra did?

'She got free,' Royce said, feeling that he was only making things worse. 'She escaped.'

Annika's lips pulled back in a viciously victorious smile.

Royce made his move. 'How was Yarra able to heal her?' he asked. 'I thought healing was the power of House Orange. And how is she able to slip through the chains even though they're made of iron?'

'Yarra can do anything. Although even for her, using magic while in contact with iron,' Annika whispered. 'She is not a criminal. She is not evil! Why won't Ray see that?'

'He must have good reason for thinking that,' he said diplomatically.

She sneered. 'Ray is only following Father's wishes.'

'If she is not a criminal,' Royce wondered, genuinely curious about this fact, about how Annika would explain it, 'then why was she in the Halls of Trepidation?'

He fully believed she was a criminal. The girl herself admitted to being a murderer. She had joined a militia, fought in long and bloody battles. But someone as good as the legends claimed should not have been caught. There had to be some other reason she ended up in the halls.

The Halls of Trepidation were the last stop for criminals. Murderers and thieves often wound up there. Terrorists and rapists were sent there the instant they were caught. No one was there by accident, and no one went there by choice. It was hell on earth, worse than hell if the demons were to be believed.

'She went there to escape the lords,' Annika said sadly. 'They banished her, but more than one wanted to see her dead. Kayneth and Joseph especially wanted her head mounted on a pike.'

'There must have been a reason.'

'Oh, there was,' she purred, 'but it didn't matter that they wanted her dead. Kayneth and Joseph never took the pledge. They don't know her importance, that she cannot be allowed to die.'

'What did she do?' he asked gently, pushing all other questions aside, questions about the pledge and her statement that Yarra could do anything.

'She killed her parents,' Annika said viciously, 'slaughtered them and their guards and the soldiers sent in to subdue her. It was a bloodbath.'

16

Pieces

A bloodbath.

Yarra had left the Cerulean Gardens, the headquarters of House Blue and main attraction of Verstra's capital, covered in the sticky, clotting blood of House Blue's personal army of guards, slaughtered them all without injuring herself in any way, and then escaped unseen by the scores of guards reacting to what they perceived to be an attack on the capital.

In the chaos, her parents had been killed – murdered, the way Annika told it – yet even after her miraculous escape, Yarra resurfaced. She did not fade into Verstra's underbelly as one would expect. She returned, was captured by the Rainbow, and tried by the convergence of lords.

For fleeing the scene of a crime, even if she had been innocent, the Rainbow would have questioned her and sentenced her to a short-time imprisonment, not in Trepidation but one of their smaller prisons, more a debriefing centre than an actual prison.

For just a single murder, she should have been sentenced to Trepidation. For the double murder of her parents and the slaughter of the countless guards that followed . . . by all rights, she should be dead. Verstran law demanded it. The law of the Rainbow demanded it.

Still, Yarra lived, had been exiled instead of executed. It didn't make any sense.

He could fully believe Yarra was capable of murdering her parents. All murderers had to start somewhere, after all. So that part of the story was believable. The part he didn't understand was how she ended up in Trepidation. If the Rainbow had banished her instead of handing down the death sentence she should have earned, how had she ended up chained inside the halls?

Head bowed, brows deeply furrowed, he stalked through the castle-like library. At one point, he rounded a corner, and Zenon fell into step beside him. The old soldier spoke in low tones, saying much of what he had expected. The girl was physically weak, damaged. No word on potential insights that could lead them to victory in this war, except he spoke with confidence, like he knew without a doubt that the girl would be crucial to their victory.

'I had her read Erryk's map,' Zenon said, 'had her make predictions based on the movements of their armies.'

'And?'

'I reset the pieces beforehand,' Zenon explained, 'moved them back two months. Positions we had assumed at the time but now know to be true.'

'And?' Royce asked again.

'And she predicted their movements almost exactly.' He said. 'I compared her predictions to the latest information we've received from the other houses. She was right.'

Royce breathed sharply through his nose, not quite a snort but almost.

'I know you think she cannot fight as part of a unit, and you may be right, but if we can utilise her magic, she could become an asset.'

'You know she is a seer?' Royce asked. Ray had given the impression that that was a closely guarded secret. His reluctance to reveal that single piece of information had been clear.

Zenon nodded. 'But she does not use that power often.'

'Why not? With that power, no one in the Rainbow need die. There would be no needless deaths. This war could be fought and won without anyone in the Rainbow shedding a single drop of blood.'

'If you want to force her to use her magic that way . . .' He shook his head. 'Ray might be the only one who could convince her to do that.'

Then Zenon peeled off and was gone. Royce kept walking through the halls, past the ruins in various state of repair, through the vast entrance hall, crossing the space with quick but still unhurried strides.

Ray and Erryk stood by the door, the latter dressed for travel and clutching in his hand a crumpled piece of paper.

'And if I can't find them?' Erryk asked.

Ray shook his head with a sigh. 'I don't want to be the one to tell her all her friends are dead. At the very least, find out what happened to Achilles.'

Erryk nodded, his slightly curly hair smothered under the dark green hood of his cloak. He fisted his hand over his heart and then raised three fingers to the sky, the House Green salute. Then Erryk took half a step back and sunk into a low mocking bow, mocking because he exaggerated the movement with great flourishes of his hands, smirked, and left with a wink.

'Who's Achilles?' he asked Ray in an undertone.

The lord sighed, ran his fingers through his hair, emerald eyes frazzled and distressed. 'Achilles is Yarra's demon hound,' he said with yet another sigh. 'He disappeared about the same time she was exiled. He was her first friend.'

Ray looked so lost, so . . . sad, Royce was struck with the uncomfortable need to comfort him.

'I would have thought you were her first friend, my lord,' he said gently.

Ray smiled grimly. 'Thanks for that, but you'd be wrong.'

He began walking down the hall, towards the study and the war room Erryk had just left vacant. Royce fell into step beside him.

'Have you changed your mind about Yarra?' Ray asked casually, his face neutral, but there was something about his tone that gave away his lingering amusement.

'Zenon reports that her physical strength is improving,' Royce said, 'but as for how useful she could be to the war effort, that remains to be seen.' Royce paused. He glanced sidelong at the lord; perhaps it would be dangerous to ask this, given how close they seemed, but he had to try. 'If she were to use her magic, then I would fully support her assistance,' he said.

'Her magic?' Ray asked.

'You said she was a seer. If she were to use those skills to aid us, to tell us of the enemy's movements and strategies, then we could outflank them, manoeuvre our own forces more efficiently. This war could be won in an instant.'

Ray's face instantly darkened. There was thunder rolling behind those emerald eyes. 'I will not use her like that,' he said evenly, the tremble in his hands giving away his anger.

Royce hid his own anger better. This . . . this brat would see them all dead. He had just refused to use what was perhaps their best chance at victory. He would send the entire Rainbow to their deaths, see them all slaughtered just to protect this one girl, this criminal, a murderer. Ray said nothing more, but it was clear he considered the matter closed.

Royce kept his anger to himself, kept his head down, kept walking. He didn't stop until he was surrounded by the suffocating presence of the disembodied library creature. This time, even the boldly lettered Keep Out sign did not faze him.

'I need to know about the butchering of House Blue's guards at the Cerulean Gardens a hundred years ago,' he said into the darkness.

Waves of rumbled laughter rolled from the shadows. Floating on their crests came a book, a ledger of crimes and the punishments doled out by the Rainbow. Tacked to the cover was a simple hand-scrawled note.

The script was almost illegible, like the hands that had formed each letter were not real hands at all but shadows and darkness condensed into solid matter, even the ink, the dark-as-darkest black ink, that made the letters swim almost liquid like over the page.

And even though they were written and thus had no audible sound associated with them, they seemed to whisper and chuckle.

'It's a good read, that,' the words proclaimed, hauntingly soft.

'Why wasn't she executed?' he asked the black.

'You cannot kill one protected by the pledge,' the voice answered.

Royce scowled. The pledge again; over and over, it was bought up yet never given an explanation. What was it, and why was it always coming up? What kind of pledge could be so powerful, so overwhelmingly binding that even the slaughtering of countless soldiers and Rainbow loyalists could not overturn it?

He grabbed a plateful of food from the kitchen before he locked himself in his room to read.

Royce dreaded reading exactly what she had done to her family, to her parents and the guards who had tried to protect them, but he had to know. It was crucial to his case, to point out to the other lords and leaders exactly what she had done and the punishment she had escaped, all so they could uphold the pledge – whatever that was.

Crime: Double murder

Description: The bodies of Ebony White and Stygian White were found nailed to the wall of their home.

Ebony White had nails through her hands and through her shoulders and neck. Her throat had been slit and the skin of her neck cut away to reveal her spine. Her eyes had been gouged out and nailed above her head like a crown. The bones of her forearms had been removed and hung from the ceiling above her. Examinations conclude that she was alive throughout the process right up until her throat was slit.

Stygian White was found nailed beside his wife, a skewer protruding from his chest. His heart had been removed and nailed to the floor at his feet. He had nails through his eyes and in his mouth and many lacerations suggesting lashings over a prolonged time. Like his wife, he had nails through his hands and shoulders, and examinations suggest he was alive until the last moment.

Culprit: Yarra White

Punishment: Banishment. Permanent expulsion from all Rainbow-related activities and affiliations. Never to have any contact with any members of the Rainbow or their associates. Forever forbidden from taking even a single step on any lands held by the Rainbow.

No word about the guards or the soldiers. But by all the gods . . . what she had done was . . . brutal. There was no other word for it. *Horrific* might have come close, but *brutal* had the harsher edge that fully encompassed the shocking feat she had achieved.

There was no escaping a crime such as that.

17

Suspicions

Yarra was acutely aware that Royce watched most of her training sessions with Zenon, knew that he watched from behind closed doors, waiting for her to reveal something or for Zenon to trip up and let slip some portion of information Royce was not supposed to know. She knew too when the eyes watching her suddenly filled with unrivalled hate, awe, fear, and no small amount of grudging respect.

'And so the cuckoo finds a worm,' she said to Zenon.

'Must be tasty,' he grunted, pulling back the bowstring of the truly huge longbow and losing an arrow that flew the length of the long room and buried itself up to the feathers in the centre of the target.

Yarra hauled on the bowstring of her own longbow, easily as huge as the one Zenon held but made all the larger by the sufficient difference in size between them. Yarra's arrow wobbled as it flew. It did not make it to the target, rather wobbled and clattered to the ground about midway between her and the target.

'How did you ever make it as an assassin, girlie?' Zenon asked.

'I wonder what he learned,' Yarra mused.

Zenon shook his head. 'I heard Annika tell him about your parents.'

Yarra's face fell. Her stone-cold eyes freezing over completely. 'I was framed,' she said.

'Aye, girlie,' Zenon said softly, 'but you weren't exactly cut up about it either.'

In the days following her first five laps around the guards' room, Zenon had had Yarra run around the perimeter of the Ivy Library until she could complete ten laps without breaking a sweat or collapsing at the end. Then they had moved on to hand-to-hand combat and then, finally, weapons.

All the while, Zenon peppered her with hypothetical questions. And Royce listened in from the shadows.

'If you were to attack the Amaranth Ruins,' he asked her, 'where would you attack from?'

'I'm an assassin,' she wheezed, drawing back another arrow, 'not some cheap oracle.'

'I know that, girlie, but you were also in a militia.'

Yarra fired – missed. 'Fine. To attack the Amaranth Ruins, you'd have to make sure House Red was otherwise occupied. The best way to do that would be to rile up the monsters in the Wild Lands or the rogue werewolves from the Maalia Mountains and get them to launch an attack on House Red.'

'And then?' Zenon prompted.

'a straight forward push from here would be best. A straight run from the Ivy Library to the Amaranth Ruins while House Red is otherwise occupied.'

'If you were to strike the Rainbow a fatal blow, what would you do?'

'Take the one thing they cannot bear to lose.'

'Aye, and what would that be?'

Yarra shot Zenon a look, dropping the bow by her side. 'Me.'

'Aye, but the monsters do not know that about us, so what would they do?'

Zenon asked question after question, patient as always and always more than happy to remind Yarra just how far behind her swordplay skills were after the years in Trepidation. He grabbed a one-handed sword and advanced.

Yarra grabbed a sword of her own and stepped into Zenon's blow. 'The Rainbow is weakest at the convergence. When all the colours come together, there is only one. And one is far easier to kill than many.'

Lunge. Parry. Slash. Dodge.

'And how would the monsters know where a convergence takes place?'

'Monsters, they may be, but stupid, they are not' was her reply.

'Girlie, please,' the old soldier begged, breathing hard and slashing at her with the sword once more, 'no riddles. I'm not in the mood.'

Yarra deflected the blow and pinned her old friend against the wall, her sword at his throat.

'Now the Rainbow is not the shadowy secret organisation it once was and should be. It is too bright for its own good. Lords and leaders and names and their lives are public knowledge to any person in Verstra willing to look. It is no secret the originals are being replaced, and although they might not know why and certainly don't know the significance of such changes, they will certainly know that there is conflict within the Rainbow. That the Rainbow is not unified.'

'So all one need do is watch an unstable house and wait until a convergence is called,' Zenon finished. 'Good job, girlie.' Zenon's face was suddenly hard. 'Now hit the target.'

Snarling, she released him, scooped up the gigantic longbow, pulled the string all the way back, and fired towards the target in a single breath, without looking. She stalked from the room, that snarl still plastered on her face.

Zenon had been right to say the monsters were not smart enough to target her. They, like most of the Rainbow, like everyone who was not a member of the original families, did not know of her importance, did not know just how much she had suffered because of her power. But there was one who did.

Zenon was one of two people outside the members of the original families to know of the pledge. The other was one of Yarra's closest friends, someone she had grown up with, experienced life's ups and downs with, someone whom, despite the differences that had forced them apart, differences that had almost destroyed both their lives, Yarra had grown to love and care for – a vampire called Jibrayne.

While they hadn't parted on the best of terms – for indeed, the last they had seen each other had been after Yarra led House Red in a crusade that had all but exterminated Jibrayne's coven, killing the only family and friends the vampire had ever known – Yarra still found it hard to believe her friend could be behind this coming war.

But somehow, impossibly, it made perfect sense, the same way her last arrow had impossibly found its mark, skewering the exact centre of the target, tunnelling through Zenon's previous arrow, splitting that perfectly in two as it went. The sudden realisation that perhaps Jibrayne was behind all these strange events – the sudden blindness of all her eyes and deafness of her ears – seemed like small steps in a much larger, beautifully enacted play for world domination. The more she thought about it, the more certain she became.

And the more she felt crushed, smothered, the more she felt that she was drowning. That the world was doing everything it possibly could to destroy the very foundation she relied on.

Jibrayne's intervention even explained the disappearance of her werewolf friend Nerys. Erryk had sent word via carrier bird yesterday. The werewolves, the ones willing to talk to him, all reported the same thing: that Nerys was gone, missing. The packs were in panic. Never had they lost a member of the council of twelve. They had even apologised for the attack on House Green, apologised and begged for forgiveness like Erryk hadn't been personally responsible for slaughtering a large number of them.

Never-friends Jibrayne and Nerys had become unlikely allies, a force for good amongst their two peoples. They kept track of each other's movements not out of concern for each other's well-being but because both knew that one wrong move from either of them could lead them both to ruin. Nerys must have known the moment Jibrayne started making any decisions that could lead to war, and Jibrayne had silenced her before the werewolf could get word to Yarra. If Jibrayne truly was behind this, the Rainbow was in more trouble than she had thought.

Jibrayne was plotting something; that much was clear. Her old friend, no doubt, planned to attack them at their weakest, with four out of the seven families left utterly defenceless against such an attack, the Rainbow would fall overnight, and after that, the world would follow. All she had to work with were three families that hated her, a further three that didn't know enough about anything to be trusted to water a pot plant, and the Mossmans, a family who meant more than the world to her, a family that was more of a family than her own had been.

They were, in short, doomed.

Always be the smartest person in the room. Sometimes she wished she wasn't.

18

Chess

'We're doomed,' Ray echoed when she told him.

'There is more than one way to win a war,' she replied, moving her pawn two places forward.

'We can't exactly ask the vampires to surrender.' Ray countered by moving his rook three places to the left.

'We could surrender the world to them, lay the entire planet at their feet. Give them everything they want. They wouldn't know what to do with it.'

'And if they want your head on a plate?'

She moved her knight forward and knocked over one of his pawns. 'Let them try and take it.'

Ray smiled tightly. 'You know very well that the pledge prevents us from allowing that to happen.'

'Too bad,' she said as his bishop snuck behind her lines and faced her king.

'Too bad for us, you mean,' Ray said edgily. 'We're the ones who'll die.'

Yarra smirked at Ray and then moved her knight to take his bishop, freeing her king.

'If only the other houses were forced to take the pledge,' she mused. 'Then you could all die together, and you wouldn't be alone.'

He moved a pawn; she moved one to block it.

'It is hard to ignore half of everything you say when what you say makes sense.'

'Isn't it?'

'But they cannot take the pledge, cannot know about it, for if they did, it would make it easier to replace us.'

'Are they so all consumed with replacing you that they would dare endanger the Rainbow to do so?'

He moved a rook, she a pawn.

'The Rainbow needs all its pieces.' She gestured to the chessboard. 'Discounting the pawns, every house can be represented by a piece.'

'But there are two rooks,' he said, moving a bishop. She took it with a pawn. 'Two knights, two bishops, a king, and a queen. How can we all be represented?'

'Fire is strong and firm,' she said. 'It rushes forward in one direction, only like a rook. Poisons too work only one way. Water is freer. It moves diagonally like the bishop, unhindered by this geometric world. Shadows are also not confined by such constraint. Air does what it pleases, jumping over problems like a knight in battle, and healing is needed everywhere at once. Fighters often let them slip by.'

Ray moved a knight, poised to strike at her queen, but Yarra only moved another pawn.

'And earth?' he asked.

'Earth stands firm, watching all, not limited in movement or fighting. But as it is the base, should it fall, there would be nothing left to fight for.'

'You're saying that I'm the king,' he said, hand hovering over his knight, ready to capture her queen.

She nodded.

Realisation dawned. 'And you are the queen,' he breathed.

'Able to do all, see all, and inhibited by nothing and no one.' She smiled at him.

Ray lowered his hand. Even in chess, the pledge must be upheld. Had she not invoked it, in her shrewd and obscure metaphoric comparison, he could have won. A flash of stone-cold eyes gleaming in triumph told him as much.

'And the pawns?' he asked.

'Have potential,' she said.

He took her rook; she moved a pawn. He took her knight; she moved a pawn.

'The pawns are our fighters, the Kayneths and Royces of the world. They do what we tell them, but they have potential.'

He cornered her king with a bishop; she placed a knight in its path. He moved a bishop of his own, she another pawn.

'One must always be weary of pawns,' she said. 'Look away, and they can become a problem. Ignore them, and they become a nuisance, but use them properly, and sometimes, sometimes they become queens.'

Yarra moved her pawn a final time, and Ray swore. Her pawn had reached the end of the board. It could progress no further. Lightly, Yarra placed a tiny paper crown on its head.

'Mate,' she said, smiling sweetly.

Ray swore again.

'Jibrayne knows,' Yarra said softly.

Ray turned to face her, saw her chew on her bottom lip and cast her head down so her midnight-black hair, gleaming like liquid night once more now that Trepidation was behind her, hid it like a curtain.

'Jibrayne knows about the pledge,' she clarified.

She looked so vulnerable like that, Ray thought, curled up in the chair as if to hide from the world.

'Jibrayne?' He racked his brain. 'That vampire you saved when we were kids? Why? How?'

'She wanted to know why your father was willing to let himself be bitten and killed if it meant even a smallest chance of escape for me.'

'And you told her?'

'I was young,' she said defensively. 'I wanted a friend who wouldn't treat me like I was about to shatter like the crystal vase I am. I wanted someone who wouldn't walk on eggshells even though they knew who I was.'

'So you told her.'

It was not a question, but she nodded.

'Everything?'

'No. But enough. The rest, she guessed. It was not hard to figure out.'

Ray considered the pledge, the wording and what it entailed. 'She plans to use this against us?' he asked.

'I am told that there is already movement afoot. The score is set with a great crescendo in mind. The tempo is rising.'

'My sources have revealed nothing.'

'Your sources' – she smirked – 'are not as good as mine. Although in this instance, my eyes seem to be blind and my ears deaf. Any more news from Erryk?'

Erryk had departed the Ivy Library solely for the purpose of tracking down the individuals loyal only to her.

'How do you even have sources?' Ray asked. 'You were in the Halls of Trepidation, for gods' sake.'

'Where do you think my sources came from? Annika was right, by the way. I only went into Trepidation to get away from the other lords.'

'Not me?'

She shook her head.

'They knew you were there,' he said. 'All of them knew where you were.'

'But they could not get to me.'

'No one willingly goes into Trepidation,' Ray said, 'and no one ever comes out. It took all seven of us, together, to get you out. Yes, we chased you. Yes, we pursued you, but, Yarra, can you blame us? We are all bound by the pledge, and you joined a militia. A militia, Yarra. You fought in wars.'

'By rights, therefore, you should all be dead already.'

'What? And leave you all alone?'

Yarra cracked a smile.

'How big a force does this vampire command?' he asked.

The smile melted from her face, and that alone was answer enough.

'Erryk has so far failed to make contact with any of the people on your list,' Ray said gently. 'You know how diligent he is. How he always makes sure to leave offerings to the nature spirits of the Ashdown Forest.'

Yarra nodded.

'Not one has agreed to speak to him. Last I heard, he was heading through the Ghost Lands.'

'And he could not find Siliba?' she asked, naming her banshee contact who lived on the outskirts of the Ghost Lands.

Ray shook his head. 'Even the ghosts would not answer him. Only one, an ancient Erryk called Romney, lingered long enough to talk.'

Yarra frowned. Located to the west of the Green Lands, the Ghost Lands were Verstra's graveyard. For such a place to be devoid of banshees, creatures that fed off death, and ghosts, creatures that were the dead, was unheard of.

Romney was the oldest ghost Yarra had ever met. He had lived through two of Verstra's great wars and witnessed three more as a ghost. Romney was nearly as old as time itself and had no reason to fear anything. For him to hide was unthinkable.

She didn't dare ask about Achilles, the demon hound she had raised from birth, didn't want to know that her oldest and closest friend could not be found.

'Again?' Ray asked.

Yarra shrugged, nodded, and waited for Ray to make the first move. 'Tell me about Royce,' she said, launching straight into an attack.

'You've met him before. Probably. I mean, I think you must have.'

Yarra frowned at him.

'When you broke out of Trepidation to see my mother, first when Annika was born and then to visit her grave the night she died. Don't deny it. I know it happened. You would have come into contact with him then. Indirectly or otherwise.' He moved a rook.

'When did he replace Zenon?'

'About fifteen years after you left, he rapidly rose through the ranks. Father loved him, praised his work ethic, said he was a better soldier than Zenon ever was.'

'That's not true,' Yarra said, moving a knight.

Ray offered her a rueful smile and captured her knight. 'That's the truth, but Father was angry you scorned us, Yarra, and that anger fuelled his rage and turned into a viciously short temper. Royce was ruthless with the other soldiers but also smart. He got himself included in every envoy we sent to another house, was given responsibilities far beyond his rank. Father even ordered Zenon to train Royce to take over, and the moment he deemed him ready, Father asked Zenon to step down.'

'He made friends with soldiers in the other houses,' Yarra continued, puzzling out the finer details for herself and moving a bishop across the board, 'probably befriended Kayneth Kor and Joseph Moon, and with the leaders of Houses Indigo and Violet on his side, probably House Orange too, his confidence no doubt soared.' Yarra speared her friend with a seething look. 'How long have you known he's been plotting to replace you?'

'Only about as long as I've been lord,' Ray said with far too much confidence, emerald eyes crinkling in amusement. He moved a knight of his own.

'Is he getting close?'

'It hardly matters how close he gets. There is no precedent for replacing members of the original families. Other leaderships were handed over because there were no other alternatives. The Amaryllis family died out, the Asters too unpredictable, the Dijon girl too young to rule on her own, and the Beryls replaced for defying the will of the council.'

'The Beryls were overthrown through majority vote,' Yarra said, beginning her ruthless attack of advancing pawns. 'If they succeeded in doing that once, are you not worried that all Royce has to do is turn all the other lords against you?'

'It is possible . . .'

Ray moved his queen. Yarra pounced with a bishop. Emerald eyes flashed in triumph as Yarra exposed her king and then narrowed in sudden concentration.

'Would Jibrayne use the conflict between lords and leaders within the Rainbow to further her own causes?'

'She most certainly would.'

'Then we better make sure we present a single united front.' Ray watched her closely, carefully chose each word. 'Royce wants to use you,' he said, 'your power. As a seer.'

'You would have me spout prophecies like a trained parrot?'

Slate-grey eyes showed no emotion. Her voice was carefully neutral.

'No, Yarra. Never. I'd never ask you to do that.'

'It's not a bad idea . . .,' Yarra mused. 'I mean, it would almost guarantee our victory.'

Ray noted the way her stone-cold eyes flashed and sparkled. 'Yarra . . . what are you planning?'

A silver sparkle and flash of ivory teeth from behind a midnight curtain of hair. 'I am an assassin, free from my chains and roaming the halls of House Green. Methinks perhaps it's time your loyal soldiers, friends old and new, remembered whom they've let loose in their home.'

19

Confrontation

R oyce left before he was discovered, leaving his shadowed hiding place as quickly as he could. He could not believe his luck. There he was, psyching himself up to ask Annika more questions about Yarra and her family when he passed the study, rarely used; he had expected the room to be empty and had been shocked but pleasantly surprised to find it occupied.

His surprise quickly turned to anger when he realised it was that troublesome girl and annoying brat lord in the room, followed by a sudden rush of suspicion. He remembered Ray stating quite clearly that the girl would remain locked up, that she was to be treated like a criminal because, to the men, she was one, yet here he was, chatting with her like they were old friends and playing what looked to be a game of chess. *Outrageous.*

The even bigger shock came when he stopped and started listening in on their conversation. He caught words like *pledge* and *Jibrayne* and *war.* The pledge, he had heard about before; it was one of the things he wanted to ask Annika, something he was even more determined to do now he had even more questions about it. He had never heard of this Jibrayne person, but if they were a vampire, particularly a living vampire, that wasn't surprising. And war, well, war was inevitable.

He snuck away as soon as he thought there was nothing more to gain from staying. Had he remained just thirty seconds longer, however, he would have seen Yarra spin towards the door and the shadows that had concealed him and would have heard her quirk an eyebrow towards Ray and ask, 'Do you think he heard?'

But Royce hurried away, back towards the training room and towards Annika, the girl who had the answers he so desperately desired.

Unfortunately, he didn't get that far. Why was it that things involving that girl were always a complicated mess? Hadn't he just left her in the study with Ray? Why was she here now raising hell with his men in the training room? And why wasn't Annika doing anything to stop it? Really, was it too much to ask her to at least look alarmed by the fighting, to at least look like she wasn't enjoying every moment of it?

How Yarra had gotten from the study to the training room faster than he had and without him noticing was currently of no consequence, nor was the fact that the fight she was engaged in seemed to have been going on for some time, judging by their laboured breaths and perspiration rates. There should have been no way she had been in the study conversing with Ray mere moments ago.

And the fighting . . . never in the weeks of training he had watched between her and Zenon had she shown this level of skill. Day after day, Zenon beat her down, pummelled her with fists and weapons, and although she was improving, never had she shown this level of skill, not in front of him. He could see how Ray could be duped into thinking her an asset.

'Beat her good!' one soldier called.

'Knock her out!'

'Teach her respect!'

Royce was half inclined to agree with his men. She needed some common sense knocked into her, and if she happened to be injured in the process, all the better. After all the beatings dished out to her, she had not broken. Perhaps, should the beating fall to the hands of his men, she would finally cave.

Royce slid his eyes to Annika, watching her with almost as much scrutiny as he watched Yarra. The smile plastered on her smooth face was not faked, not entirely. Her sharp emerald eyes scanned every movement, every sword stroke, catching the feint Yarra almost fell for and the downward slice that almost took off her head. It took Royce a few moments to realise it, but the closer Yarra came to being injured, the stiller Annika held herself, the more tension built up in her body.

It was like Annika was more worried about the girl's life than the girl herself. Because Yarra, stupid, haughty Yarra, was fighting without a care in the world. She showed blatant disregard for the soldier's skill, showed little to no skill herself, just flung herself recklessly over and over again into the blows, the parries, and the thrusts.

But for all her recklessness, she was winning, the haphazard blows strung together in a flawless pattern, the unnecessary twirls and flourishes she threw in at every opportunity making her look like she was dancing. It was fascinating – terrifying but fascinating.

Then one of the soldiers shouted out the last straw. 'Kill her!'

Annika went still, her eyes shuttered. Not a fraction of a second later, she had sprung forward, pushed through the circle of onlookers, and was levelling twin rapiers at the warring combatants.

'*Enough!*' she roared.

Yarra froze instantly, her short daggers (where had she got those?) hanging limp from her hands and then clattering to the ground. The soldier she faced, Royce's chief strategist, the most senior member under Zenon and Royce himself, did not. The soldier's large one-and-a-half-handed sword swung in a dangerous arc straight towards Yarra's unprotected neck. Yarra didn't do a thing to stop it, didn't so much as flinch.

'*I said enough!*'

Yarra didn't move, but the soldier's sword didn't decapitate her. The blade stopped a hair from her skin, halted in place by a thin vine grown with great haste and great care from the floor beneath her.

'No one is to die,' Annika said, a hand outstretched towards the vine, a sheen of sweat covering her brow. 'Have I made myself clear?'

'Y-yes, ma'am,' the soldier stammered out.

Yarra snapped her fingers, a bored smile playing about her lips, and the vine shattered like glass. The sword remained poised by her neck until she levelled the soldier with a stone-cold unflinching stare, and he dropped it by his side.

'I am an assassin,' Yarra said. 'I have killed people and fought in wars. I have infiltrated your home and broken free of your prison.' She spun in a circle, arms wide. 'So please, point a sword at me if it makes you feel better.'

Twenty blades faced her in an instant.

'No fighting!' Annika snapped. 'I forbid it.'

'She is a criminal,' a guard protested, 'a murderer. She should be locked up, chained.'

'I will not have my brother's entire guard slaughtered simply because you would feel safer with her in chains!'

'Don't be ridiculous, Annika,' Yarra said in a lilting sing-song voice. 'I wouldn't kill all of them.'

'She wouldn't be able to kill all of us,' one soldier called, 'right?'

Annika flashed her teeth in what could have been half a smile.

'The queen offers you a choice,' Yarra said, eyes flashing towards Royce with a menacing glint. 'Send a champion to face the queen or feel the wrath of the assassin you let into your home. Win, I will consent to be chained. Lose, and I remain free.'

'Who is the queen?' someone dared ask into the stunned silence.

Royce knew why she was smiling now and felt cold dread settle inside him. She knew he had been listening, had said what she did not only to answer Ray's questions but also to entice *him*, to keep *him* latched on the scent of her mystery – and it had worked. *Damn her.*

'She is the queen,' he said, 'the queen who sees all, knows all, and is stopped by no one and nothing.'

Yarra sketched a bow, low and mocking.

'I cannot allow this,' Annika said, wringing her hands in frustration and shaking her head so hard, her pigtails and the many frilly ruffles of her dress swished from side to side.

'I promise I will use only the daggers,' Yarra said, rolling her eyes, 'nothing more. Scout's honour.'

Annika looked around the room, at the ring of soldiers all levelling swords and blades in her direction, trapping her inside with Yarra, and threw her hands up in defeat. 'Fine,' she said, holding out her hand. 'Do whatever you want.'

Yarra stared at her outstretched hand and did not move. Annika flapped her fingers impatiently.

'Hand it over.'

'I won't use it.'

'Hand it over.'

Green and grey eyes stared each other down. Finally, reluctantly, Yarra reached a hand up to her head and pulled off her crown. *Crown* was perhaps the wrong word for it. It was more of a headband or a braided rope wrapped around itself and balanced atop her midnight head. Either way, it was not until Yarra took it off and handed it over to Annika that he realised what it was.

It was a whip, curled into a tight circle with barbed ends, giving it a very crown-like appearance. There was no doubt what it was now – Myrthos, her weapon of choice. Annika had just disarmed the last remaining member of House White and left her alone in a circle of angry, scared men with swords drawn.

'Who wishes to challenge the queen?'

Royce knew he would regret this for the rest of his days, but . . . 'I will.'

Men parted like the sea as he approached. Annika stood between them, a look of deep disapproval on her face. She held out a hand, Yarra on her left, Royce on her right, and looked them both in the eye.

'This is a terrible idea,' she muttered. 'Begin.'

'Wait!' Royce called. 'We should fight evenly. Without magic.'

'There is no magic that can be used fast enough to aid in a sword fight between masters,' Annika said with a slightly disgusted sideways sneer. It was like she couldn't believe he dared speak up to her.

'Yarra is a seer,' Royce said matter-of-factly. 'If a fair fight is to be had, her magic must be suppressed so she cannot read my movements beforehand.'

'Any of your magic grants you swiftness,' Yarra shot back. 'The scales would be balanced.'

'To see the future is a far greater advantage,' Royce said, not daring to ask how, exactly, she knew what his magic was.

Annika looked to Yarra. The girl merely shrugged.

'If you insist,' she said and then turned to Zenon. 'Bracelet me.'

Zenon did not move.

'I know you have them,' the girl trilled. 'I know you've carried them ever since they got me out of Trepidation. Hand them over.'

The old soldier scowled but produced a pair of wooden bangles wrapped in swirling whorls of metal. He carried them to the girl, showing them to Royce as he did, and then fastened them around Yarra's slim wrists.

Royce balked at the wrongness the bracelets caused in him. The wood was Rowan ash; the metal was iron. The bracelets combined the two magic nullifying substances. Just one bracelet would have been enough to suppress his magic or the magic of any of his soldiers. Yarra had two, and after closer inspection of the many faded scars on her wrists – scars that ran ladders up the lengths of both forearms, almost like she'd made many of them herself – the way those bracelets seemed to fit perfectly with the oldest and deepest of the scars . . . she had worn them before at length.

She raised an eyebrow. Royce nodded.

'Begin!' Annika called again.

Royce had her pinned in a moment. Before the breath had even left Annika's lips, he had grabbed a two-handed sword and swung it with deadly force towards the girl, angling the blade down so as to cut deep into her neck and collarbone, doing as much damage as he could. Royce was swinging before Yarra even had time to hear the end of Annika's words, swinging that great blade with a follow-through to cleave straight through bone.

He may had claimed to want a fair fight, had even had her magic stifled. But that didn't mean he would refrain from using magic.

Only the swing went on too long, the arc too long. The point where he should have made contact with Yarra's flesh came and went, and still, his sword sailed through clean air. Momentum bought him forward, unbalanced as he was; he stumbled, hurriedly attempting to get his feet under him once more. And still, his sword sailed through the air.

The final jarring impact, he felt through his teeth, gritting them to stop them splitting. This also had the adverse effect of smothering the grunt of pain that surged from within him. The clang that echoed throughout the training room rang in utter silence.

Royce blinked through the pain, glaring at the tears that sprang to his eyes. His sword had not hit Yarra; rather, it had hit the floor, the ground where she, by all rights, should have been. No one had the right to move that fast. Not even he could move that fast, even aided by magic. There was no way she could have seen him move. Even he had not decided on this pre-emptive attack until the last minute. There was no way she should have had enough time to react and dodge.

Hastily, he scanned the room, took in the stunned faces of his men, the guards who no doubt knew what he had attempted and were just as surprised as he was that it failed, Annika, face impassive and full of disapproval. If not for the slight glint in her emerald eyes, a glint that seemed to be laughing at him, he might have thought she hadn't seen anything.

He scanned the whole room and couldn't for the life of him see the girl. He half hoped she had run away. The sensible part of him knew that was impossible, but still . . . one could hope.

'Don't kill him,' Annika said, her voice both exasperated and amused.

Royce felt it then, the thin pressure at his neck, on both sides of his neck, and the presence behind him that definitely hadn't been there a heartbeat earlier.

Twin daggers poised to remove his head from his neck. Yarra loomed over him. His overpowered swing had left him unbalanced; his stumble had caused him to fall, and as a result, he was on one knee – a rookie error. Where before, it would have been impossible for Yarra to decapitate him in one blow, now, with his head closer to her level, she not only had a chance but was also poised to use it.

Yarra loosed a heavy sigh. 'I'm not gonna kill him. We haven't had our fair fight yet.'

The way she stressed 'fair' set his teeth on edge. It told him that she not only knew he had technically cheated by swinging early and using magic but also had allowed it, planned for it, and turned it to her advantage.

Yarra released him, and he climbed to his feet, glaring at her all the while. She danced half a step back and bent into a bow, a mocking bow, lowering her head, exposing the back of her neck like she had nothing to fear, like she knew he could not strike fast enough to make the most of this opening she had just given him. Royce scowled, baring his teeth in a growl.

Yarra raised her head and smiled, cold eyes flashing. She took up a defensive stance, twin daggers poised before her. The dagger in her left hand was held across her face, the silver of the blade as uncaring as the grey of her eyes. The dagger in her right hand, she held in a backhanded grip, angling it away from her. Royce took up a stance of his own, still scowling.

They squared off, the moments dragging longer and longer. Royce was determined not to move first, but Yarra was still as stone, her eyes just daring him to take another swing at her. He broke first.

Surging forward in a blast of motion, he hefted the sword up above his head and bought it down with a clash onto her dagger. She deflected it, choosing not to meet the blow head on but to pass his blade down the length of her own and fling the tip off point.

That was with her right hand. With her left, she stabbed at his shoulder, twirling clockwise so her momentum carried her around and behind him. Royce spun and slashed, feinted to the left, and stabbed for her head. She fell for the feint but still managed to avoid dying by ducking under his blow.

Two double feints in quick succession, aiming for her legs and then her ribs – she twirled out of the way of each, twisting and twirling with such grace, it was almost like she was dancing, her daggers an extension of her being. They blocked Royce at every turn, and it seemed almost as if she wasn't trying.

Then she was crouching, swords out like spines of some great beast, and Royce found himself flat on his back on the floor, a foot-shaped bruise forming on his chest and the world spinning.

'This is no fun,' Yarra declared. 'The queen broadens her challenge to all. Come at me, all of you.'

'Yarra, no!' Annika cried.

'Don't tell me you're all scared,' she cooed, 'that you're all too afraid to face me.'

'Yarra, you are the last of House White! You cannot do this!' Annika was almost crying from exasperation.

'Don't tell me you're all scared of one little girl –'

'Yarra, *stop!*'

'One single lone girl? Is that too much for you?'

Annika grabbed at her arm, wrestled one dagger away from her. Yarra threw her aside, spinning and laughing maniacally.

'As a member of the ruling family, I forbid you from touching her until I return!' she barked. Then the young Mossman sprinted from the room.

'Look at you all. Brave soldiers stumped by the likes of one single frail girl. A girl who spent the last fifty years in the halls of Trepidation. A girl who is thin and frail and weak.'

Annika burst back into the room, Ray right behind her.

'Will you fight me now?' Yarra challenged. When none of the men moved, even though it was clear many of them wanted to, she flipped her remaining dagger in her hand. 'Will you fight me now?'

Before any of them could move, she brought it down on herself, skewering her right hand clean through the palm.

20

Crisis

Blood sprayed. Men screamed. Soldiers recoiled in shock and revulsion. Annika screamed. Ray surged forward. Royce just watched, eyes wide.

The lord of House Green stopped just short of the girl. He towered over her. His eyes were calm in the face of her wide and crazed expression, the half tilt of her mouth that showed no humour, only deranged joy. The hand that still gripped the hilt of the dagger shook slightly. Blood splattered on the floor, the only sound before the crack.

The crack of his skin on hers. The crack that snapped her head sideways as he slapped her.

'Stop it,' he said quietly, too quietly.

Yarra blinked. 'The king will not stop the queen.'

'The game can still be won without a queen,' Ray countered.

'Prove it,' she snapped. 'Fight me.'

'No.'

Yarra withdrew the dagger with a sickening squelch from her hand and placed it at her own throat, right where her pulse throbbed.

'Fight me or I cut it.'

Ray was almost shaking with rage, but he spooled it into himself, reeled himself back from that brink and faced her with deadly calm, a balm against her rabid, almost deranged grinning.

'No.'

This time, when blood sprayed, Royce had been expecting it.

Ray did not flinch as her blood sprayed over his face, neck, and chest, did not even lift a hand to wipe it away. He merely reached out a hand

and grabbed her wrist, twisted it until she was forced to drop the dagger, glared at her. He held her like that, suspended by one arm as his free hand plugged the tear in her throat and the life blood that sought freedom.

'Heal,' he hissed through his teeth.

She shook her head.

'Heal,' he said again, voice breaking as a sob choked past his lips.

Royce spun, expecting to see Annika in a similar state of panic. From what he had gathered, she was someone important to them. If she were to die – and she most certainly was about to die – they would undoubtable be hurt, maybe hurt enough to get careless in their judgement, enough to allow him to assume control, to pose a successful takeover. *Maybe.*

Annika was nowhere to be found.

Yarra shook her head. 'I refuse,' she whispered, voice weak and gluggy.

'Heal, Yarra,' Ray begged. He begged. 'Heal yourself. Please.'

She shook her head. 'If the queen is not needed . . .' She trailed off.

Ray shook her, shaking her like a doll, his hand still clamped to her neck. But he failed to stem the flow of blood.

They may have immortal lifespans, be blessed with almost unending life, but they could still die. They still aged, could still be injured, could still get hurt, and could still die. Yarra could not have healed herself anyway. The bracelets she wore stifled her magic.

'*Yarra!*' Ray shouted, shaking her. '*Yarra!*'

Ray was crying, sobbing her name over and over, roaring it at the top of his voice as if volume alone could bring her back. But she was limp, swaying in his grip, even as the torrent of blood continued to cascade down her body.

'*Yarra!*' a shrill voice echoed through the training room.

This voice too was choked with tears, but it was more terror-stricken than Ray's. It instantly drew all eyes to it. Ray spun instantly, Yarra a dead weight in his arms.

Royce turned to face Annika, her tear-streaked face, the pigtails pulled askew, the blood-splattered dress. Something else was wrong. Something else had happened.

'It's Kelly . . .,' Annika choked out. 'She's . . . she's . . .'

Stone-cold eyes cracked open, lips pulled back in a slight sneer, but she made no sound as Ray carried her, swift as the wind, through the library after his youngest sister.

Royce burst into the room after his lord. The sight that met his eyes was nothing short of horrific.

Except *horrific* was becoming a relative term. The aftermath of the werewolf fight had been horrific. The girl's injuries after he had dragged her through the forest had been horrific. This was too, in a way.

Matt was crouched over Kelly, his creamy hair flecked with blood, his shoulders heaving with the force of his sobs. Kelly, if anything, looked worse than she had in the immediate aftermath of the werewolf attack. The slice on her face had reopened and was cascading blood into her golden hair. The bite marks on her left arm looked fresh, and she was panting short shallow breaths, like it was hard for her to get enough air.

Matt looked up as Ray entered, Yarra in his arms. His eyes immediately went to her, pleading.

'S-she was t-trying t-t-to use "growth" o-on herself. J-just t-to see if it, it would work. B-bu-but . . .'

'Growth' was the name of the most common earth magic spell. It encouraged living things to grow faster than nature would normally allow. Clearly, the magic had reacted badly to Kelly's injuries. Ray held Yarra out before him, once again holding her up by just her arm. He had even released the pressure he had had on her neck. Yarra swung her head around like it was on a swivel and glared at Ray over her shoulder.

'Please help her,' Matt begged, tears and snot running down his face, 'please.'

Cold, hard, unimpressed eyes surveyed the scene before her, Kelly, Matt, Annika, even Royce and the few soldiers who had followed him before finally resting with disdain on Ray again. Her very eyes seemed to scream, *Seriously?*

Ray broke first, as Royce had now come to expect when it came to her, that girl, whoever she was.

'I am not above using my family to ensure your survival,' he said tightly, 'not when I know you will do anything to save them.'

Yarra swayed as he dropped her but did not fall, still staring at him with such loathsome hate. Royce felt uncomfortable being in the same room. She tottered over to Kelly. Yarra turned her stare on Matt.

'There is only one person who could have convinced her to do something as extreme as this,' she said as her hand began to glow and the blood still pouring from both of them lessened. 'Only one person could convince her to go to such lengths, and even then, she only would have done it because she knows that if my life were lost, it would mean the end of yours as well.'

Matt paled.

'So clever,' Yarra sang, flesh knitting together on her hand and on Kelly. 'So, so clever. Damn you for ruining all my fun.'

'The pledge prevents us from allowing you to die,' Ray said in a hard voice. 'We are to keep you alive, even if it means our deaths.'

'it is our job to protect you, Yarra,' Kelly said softly, struggling to rise as the last of her injuries knitted together, 'even if we have to protect you from yourself.'

'You would be the first to think that way,' Yarra muttered.

Shame coloured all emerald eyes in the room. None of them said a word.

Yarra stood, her own injuries having healed, and scowled at them all. 'How did you have time to plan all this? To plan and plot and scheme with the best of them? So clever. So, so clever,' she said. 'I only decided to challenge the guards after we finished playing chess.'

'Despite what you may think, Yarra,' Ray said, 'your actions are quite easy to predict.'

21

Pledge

The situation defused, and calm once again returned to the dynamics of House Green. Royce could see no better time to ask one of his more pressing questions, especially now that it had been bought up again, right in front of him.

'What is the pledge?' he asked.

Yarra rounded on him. She didn't move physically, but Royce was suddenly very aware of their positions – or the fact that the Mossmans had just collectively revealed that they valued the life of this girl over their own. There would be no chance of him getting to her now, not that there ever had been. He realised that now. He glanced quickly at her wrists, where she still wore those Rowan ash and iron bracelets. She shouldn't have been able to use magic at all with those on.

'You,' Yarra accused, 'have been a very bad boy.' She continued in a sing-song voice, dancing and twirling around the Mossmans. 'Somebody went to the Library.'

The four of them paled.

'You didn't.' Kelly whispered.

'You shouldn't have,' Ray said. 'It's forbidden.'

'Why?' Annika asked.

Matt spoke in the quietest voice of all. All he asked was 'Did you see it?'

They all seemed to be waiting for an answer, but Royce had none to give. Instead he simply asked, 'It?'

'There is a reason we forbid guards and soldiers, even branch families, from going into the library wing,' Ray said softly.

'There is a thing in there,' Annika said, 'a-a creature.' She shuddered violently.

Royce thought of the disembodied voice, of the smothering sensation he had felt amongst the shelves and shelves of books. He had wondered what the voice was. Now he supposed he was about to find out.

'How did you know he was there?' Ray asked Yarra.

The girl shrugged. 'He told me.'

Ray looked outraged. '*You went to see him?*'

Yarra nodded.

'Doesn't he want you dead?' Kelly asked.

Another nod.

'Who is he?' Royce asked, almost fearing the answer.

'A creature of ancient times long past,' Matt said, 'a monster trapped in the library by our ancestors and the White. The Rainbow's last line of defence for the books should House Green ever fall.'

'A monster?'

'His name is Nifilious,' Yarra said, not meeting the emerald eyes of the Mossmans. 'He claims to be a god, but really, what god would lose a game of cards to a child?'

'And he wants you dead?' Royce asked, feeling the need to make completely, absolutely sure he understood what was going on.

'Well, of course, he wants me dead,' Yarra said, her words dripping sarcasm. 'I beat him at cards. As a result, he is now bound by the pledge. Same as the others.'

'And the pledge is . . . ?' he prompted.

'Secret,' Ray snapped. 'The pledge is secret.'

'Oh, why bother trying to hide it now? He practically knows already.' Yarra waved her hand dismissively. 'Go ahead. I give permission for you to spill the secrets long kept by the founders alone or whatever. Just tell him already.'

'The pledge is sacred, Yarra,' Kelly said.

'To you, maybe. Not to me. I never asked for this.'

'The pledge is sacred,' Ray repeated. 'If you wish to tell him, then go ahead, but I will have no part in it.'

Ray up and left, Matt and Kelly quick to follow. Annika took a moment to glare at them both before she followed. Royce wished they hadn't left him alone with the girl. She made him uncomfortable.

'Walk with me,' she said, 'and I will tell you about the pledge and the curse it has placed upon my family.'

Royce kept silent, not believing his luck.

'The Rainbow is comprised of seven houses,' Yarra said, 'seven houses for the seven colours of the rainbow, but above them all, there is another. Much like how visible light can be split into seven colours, the original seven people, the people who became the founders of each house, were all the product of one family. The offspring, if you will, of one great, all-ruling family – the White.

'This first generation, the founders, each took up a specific role in the defence of this world from the monsters and demons that sought to make it their own. Red took up war. Orange, healing. Yellow took up the mantle of communication, ensuring all houses remained in contact and maintained the ability to work together. Green became the keepers of knowledge. Blue became the peacekeepers, the law the others and the world must answer to. Indigo studied poisons and toxins, both to make their own forces immune and as acts of chemical warfare against the toughest of demons. And Violet became spies, keeping everyone informed of the monsters' goings-on.

'The seven of them formed the Rainbow, an organisation to protect from the shadows and rule from afar. They became all powerful, controlled everything. Nothing went on without the Rainbow's knowledge, and above them all was the White.

'It was a time of great chaos for the demons and monsters of the world. They were hunted and had nowhere to hide. So they lashed out. The founders were too well protected, but the White were not. They were a small family, as families went, but powerful. The demons laid siege to their home for three hundred years before they broke through and slaughtered them all.

'The founders were devastated. Of course, they were devastated. Losing a parent is always hard. But they quickly noticed a lapse in their own power. The magic they commanded was not as strong, more easily overcome by the demons, until finally, it failed them altogether. The Rainbow, so newly formed and brimming with potential, was crushed, the founders and their families forced into hiding, and the reign of demons began anew.

'They did not give up though. No, those founders were tough. Resilient. Violet had heard rumours that there were survivors of the White hiding in the mountains, you see, for although the White were not a large family, they were adventurous. For them, living on a mountain would have posed no real challenge. The founders scoured the world, hiked up every mountain to find them. And when they did, they made the pledge.'

Listening with rapt attention, Royce took a moment to realise she had stopped talking. He glanced over at her, wondering.

'Why?' he asked. 'And what exactly is the pledge?'

Yarra pushed open the door, and Royce stepped inside without thinking. The smothering, suffocating presence he felt instantly told him he was once again in the library, surrounded by the walls and shelves and books that all seemed alive with the same monstrous presence he now knew was Nifilious.

'And so the White returns to the Halls of Green,' the voice cooed. 'Care for a rematch, devil spawn?'

'Maybe later, Nifilious,' Yarra said. 'I know you've already met Royce here, but let me make formal introductions. Royce, this is Nifilious, Nifilious, this is Royce.'

'Charmed,' the voice said curtly. 'Well, devil spawn, if you're not here to release me, then get lost.'

'As a matter of fact, I am here to release you.'

The library seemed to freeze, like Nifilious was so shocked, he simply forgot to breathe. Royce wondered absently if he even needed to. If he truly was a god, did he need to breathe?

'Nifilious, I release you from your oath. I temporarily give you permission to talk freely about me and mine.'

Suspicion clear and thick in his voice, he asked, 'Why?'

'Royce here wants to know about the pledge, and I want you to tell him all about it. I know you gave him information on the other houses, and I want you to make available the books on my ancestors and on myself if they still exist.'

'If ever there was a book that was, its information is held in here. Such is the task I am charged with. That and the pledge.'

Yarra smiled at the darkness, stone-cold eyes burning bright like pinprick stars. But she seemed different. He realised with a shock that she had not spoken in riddles. All the time she spoke to him about her family, she had not uttered a single riddle. It made her suddenly seem imposing, like a fortress with all its defences up and proudly on display.

It also unfroze the ice from her eyes. For the first time since he had met her, her eyes seemed more silver than grey.

But it also made her seem weaker somehow. Beneath the fortress-like aura, he felt he could see her arms wobble slightly, her shoulders shake as if she was cold. And steam, actual steam hissed around those Rowan ash and iron bracelets she still wore, curling and rising to shroud her too-pale face in ethereal light.

The image he had formed of her after reading what she had done to her parents did not gel with what he saw now, nor did it fit with the personality she had shown during her weeks of training with Zenon. He had no doubt she was capable of killing, had no doubt she had actually been the one to end her parents' lives, but the way she had done it . . . the brutality described in the incident report – that was not her, not from what he had seen. *Interesting.*

'I wonder if Erryk's sent any more letters,' Yarra said absently. She waggled her fingers in a very patronising wave and breezed back through the door, swaying slightly as she went. 'Have fun!' she called.

Royce shifted from foot to foot, not quite sure what had happened or what to make of his new revelations – or why Yarra had left him here, alone.

'is the oath she just released you from the same pledge that binds the Mossmans?' he asked.

'You're not stupid,' Nifilious said. 'Good. Tell me what you think the pledge is. What have you learnt?'

Royce scowled at the darkness and the voice it concealed. 'I know that it's something the founders created after they were all nearly wiped out. Something to ensure their own powers remained intact and at their peak. My guess would be that the pledge is to protect members of House White. To keep them alive so that the powers of the founders and their descendants did not diminish.'

'Ahhh, the founders. I remember them, so misguided, so untamed. In essence, you are correct.' Nifilious said bitterly. 'In actual fact, there is more to it than that.'

'What do you mean?' Royce asked. 'Surely, just keeping the Whites alive would be enough to secure their power.'

'Think about why the seven most powerful individuals of their time would need to make a pledge such as the one you have just described.'

Royce frowned. Nifilious was right. It didn't make sense. Why would the founders of the Rainbow need to pledge themselves to protect the White? What was so important about them? Surely, the Rainbow would be stronger without the dangers the pledge placed on them.

The Rainbow had flourished. The Rainbow was unbreakable. It was the ultimate defence for Verstra against the monsters. That was why he had planned his takeover so carefully. He wanted the transition to be as seamless as possible so the Rainbow's strength remained intact, especially with war brewing.

In ancient times, there would have been even greater threats of war. The Rainbow would have needed to be even stronger. So why had the founders and all their descendants pledged themselves to protect a family as wild and as dangerous as the White?

'Yarra must have told you something about her family. Surely,' Nifilious prompted.

'No . . .,' Royce said. 'She didn't . . .'

'Smart but slow. Not the best combination, but we each take what we can get.'

Royce glared into the gloom. 'She said the Whites were adventurous,' he said at last.

'Suicidal, more like.'

Given what he had just seen, what had just transpired, Royce had to agree. The girl had just slit her own throat to prove a point, had challenged a room full of highly skilled soldiers who all thought she was a criminal with a smile on her face. She was certifiably crazy. And the Mossmans hadn't seemed surprised by her behaviour in the slightest – had planned for it, in fact.

'Think about who she is,' the ancient god drawled impatiently, 'about what she can do.'

Royce shook his head with a loud sigh. He began pacing the shelves of books, not looking at any of the titles but just thinking.

'She is a seer,' he said to no one in particular. 'I've never met another seer before. If the White were a family of seers, it would make sense to protect them, to keep them on side.'

The founders must have wanted to use their power to gain the upper hand against the demons, much like he wanted to do in this war. But that didn't explain how they ended up being slaughtered all those years ago. Surely, if the Whites were a family of seers, they would have been able to foresee the three-hundred-year siege that had killed them all and avoided it.

'But Yarra can also turn to shadows,' Royce continued. 'I've seen her do it. Multiple times. It's how she continually manages to escape her chains.'

Nifilious made a rumbling sound. Royce ignored it.

'But all her chains are designed to nullify magic. Those bracelets look as though they were made specifically for her, to nullify whatever her magic truly is. But they don't work. Or she has too much power for the combination of both Rowan ash and iron to smother. Is that possible?'

'What else do you know about her?' Nifilious asked.

'She was not killed by poison,' Royce said, ignoring Nifilious. 'Ray said that was because poison was a part of her nature. He said it the same way he might have described earth as being a part of his own being.'

'And what does that tell you?'

'Poison is the domain of House Indigo, shadows the powers of House Violet –' Royce felt himself go cold.

The Rainbow was Verstra's most powerful magic organisation. The seven houses each held ultimate dominion over one aspect of magic. But if the founders were all the children of one family, the Whites . . . and if that family had survived to this day . . .

No wonder they had pledged themselves to protect her.

'What is she?' he asked softly.

Nifilious was silent.

'What is she?' he asked again.

The Rainbow relied on its members' magic to keep the monsters at bay. The founders had allowed the Whites to be slaughtered, and their magic had dwindled as a result. Why, if not to assure that magic continued to exist?

'What is she?'

'I think you know,' Nifilious purred.

Royce knew there was no blood in his face, knew he must look as pale as Yarra, was probably shaking as much as she had been too.

'We pledge to protect the White and all their members,' Annika said softly, entering the library. Her smooth face was very pale, her emerald eyes wide in terror. 'We pledge to keep them from harm. To be both their sword and shield.'

'Why?' Royce asked, although he knew. He knew why. He just had to hear her say it.

'Because without the White, there would be no Rainbow,' Annika said. 'The Whites have had no real power within the Rainbow for centuries, aside from the power they give us, the direct descendants of the founders. We pledge to protect them because without them, the Rainbow would fall, even if they haven't actively participated in any way, shape, or form for more generations than I can count. We protect them, for without them, there is no future for us.'

'It took generations for the founder's children to curb that adventurous spirit,' Nifilious said, to Annika's clear horror. 'Generation after generation of White descendants were protected and sheltered. Kept from harm and deprived of the one thing they loved. It is true in the past, the White family was adventurous. It was that adventure that kept them sane. The power to see the future is a heavy burden to bear. They coped by testing its limits. By seeing how far they could push themselves before they saw their own deaths. Deprived of that, they became lost. Their families became smaller and smaller, their power more and more unstable.'

'We pledge to put their lives before our own,' Annika said, 'but as long as they still breathed, they meant nothing as people to our ancestors.'

'That little she-devil is the first in nearly twelve generations of Whites to take up a sword and fight in any capacity,' Nifilious said.

'A fact that makes her all the harder to protect,' Annika said, 'but at least she is happy.'

'The she-devil will be the end of you,' the voice said.

Annika shuddered.

'What do you mean?' Royce asked.

Annika let out a low laugh, the sound creepily echoed by Nifilious. 'We pledge to protect her against all odds,' she said, 'the downside of which is the fact that if a member of the White dies, the family directly responsible for not keeping them alive dies as well. If Yarra were to die while she was in our care, the lives of every single Mossman would be forfeit.'

'And as Yarra is the last living descendant of the White . . .' Nifilious trailed off, a smile plain in his voice.

'As Yarra is the last White, not only would the lives of House Green be ended, but so too would the lives of every other house be forfeit as well. That is the price we each pay for pledging ourselves to her.'

'My life too, I suppose,' Nifilious mused. 'Of course, I didn't willingly pledge to protect her. She tricked me into it, but it binds me as tightly as it binds Little Ms Annika here.'

'So now you know,' Annika said. 'Now you know a secret that should never have been told. A secret to destroy the world.'

Royce faced her in silence. His favourite Mossman, the fierce little girl who hated and loved with equal brutal passion, now levelled him with such an unguarded questioning look that he paused. He could use this to destroy them, them and the other families that remained in power. He could use this to spearhead his takeover, use this to destroy her brother, and she knew it.

'So now you know,' she said. 'What will you do?'

22

Contingent

Yarra knew Ray would hate her. After what she had just done, how could he not? They had concluded that Royce could bring down the three remaining original families and effectively force a complete restructure of the Rainbow. They had concluded that that would be bad, that Jibrayne would use that internal chaos to attack to devastating effect.

And she had not just given him fuel for the fire but also handed him the smoking gun. Ray had to hate her.

But it was not all bad. There was a plus side. That was why she'd done it, not out of any hate for Ray or his family or hatred for the Rainbow in general despite what they had done to her. She had done it to save them all, to save them.

If Jibrayne succeeded in her attack and the world fell, then the monsters – the werewolves and ghosts, nymphs and sirens, all of them – would fall as well. This world was home to all of them. There had to be a way to save them.

Only the Rainbow, united, had that sort of power. Only all seven of the original families united with the White had any hope of saving them all. Yarra was the last descendant of the White, Ray and his siblings all that remained of the Mossman legacy. The other houses were in even worse states.

Surely, her family, however docile and tamed they had become, had not allowed an original family to simply die out. Her mother had always hinted at her true role in the Rainbow, hinted at it but never made any move, never acted outside her role as glorified prisoner.

'I'm working to set things right, Yarra,' her mother had told her over and over. 'Things will not be as they were.'

However often she said it, however, it made little difference. Yarra didn't believe her. She had never done anything to change her own circumstances or intervene in the goings-on of the Rainbow. Only Yarra had dared go that far. And look where that had gotten her – exiled and hated, a prisoner her whole life.

Yarra knew more about the Rainbow than anyone, knew more about it than the people running it even. She had delved into the Rainbow's past, learned its secrets, and uncovered more than one conspiracy past lords had died to bury. She had practically grown up in House Green, the keeper of all knowledge, locked and chained inside its walls, had befriended and tricked the ancient and timeless creature that inhabited their library, the treasure trove of their entire history, and learned it all.

That had birthed Rule One. She had stuck to it since.

She had to have read something somewhere, learned something that could help her. There had to be. Yarra searched her brain, peered through each and every memory, no matter how painful, pieced together what she knew of the Rainbow, what she knew of each house, and what she knew about each of the original families.

She walked into the soldiers' training room, brows furrowed.

'Lookie here, boys,' one of the soldiers cooed. 'Little Ms Perfect here is back for another beating.'

The frown she raised to meet his gaze was one of mocking confusion. 'Another beating?' she asked sweetly. 'I don't understand. I won. Didn't I win? I think I won. I must have won. Didn't I?'

'You lost,' the soldier spat, 'fair and square.'

'But we didn't even get to finish our fight.'

'When Lord Mossman interfered, you were almost dead. Royce was not. The win is his.'

Yarra sneered. 'OK, so technically, that might be true, but I never specified the match would end in death –'

'Fair's fair, girlie,' Zenon said, pushing through the other soldiers to stand at their head. 'Consent to be chained, like you promised.'

'I promised that?' she asked.

Zenon glared at her and in front of his fellow soldiers, all of whom hated her and wanted nothing more than to see her dead at their feet. She had no chance.

'Fine!' she snapped. 'But this is not over. I'm still an assassin. I could still beat each and every one of you. Murder you in your sleep if I wanted.'

'Yeah, yeah,' Zenon said, gripping her arm tightly and practically dragging her from the room. 'Sure, you could.'

As Zenon hauled her from the room, she twisted in his grasp and sneered at the soldiers. 'I want a rematch!' she shrieked at them.

'Are you quite done, girlie?' Zenon hissed, gripping her arm tighter.

Yarra let out a small yelp and mutely nodded. They rounded a corner, and Zenon marched her down the corridor – fast. They walked another several hundred metres until they rounded a final corner and approached her cell, but he did not throw her into it. No, Zenon swung her around and slammed her into the door.

'*What were you thinking?*' he hissed, face pressed so close to hers, spit sprayed her cheek. 'Do you have any idea what you've done? *Do you have any idea what Royce could do with that kind of information?* How long he's been searching for something, anything to take Ray down? What in all the hells possessed you to tell him about the pledge?'

'If it was going to happen sooner or later, better sooner, when we can prepare for it and deal with the damage in a quick and timely fashion. And if Jibrayne really is building an army and if she really does plan on attacking the Rainbow when all the lords and leaders are at one another's throats, better sow the seed of discord now than let Jibrayne do it later.'

'You will ruin him,' Zenon said.

'I know.' Yarra didn't meet his eyes. 'But I will save the world.'

Zenon released her, fastened fresh iron chains around her wrists above the Rowan ash bracelets she still wore, and threw her into the cell. 'I hope you know what you're doing,' he said.

'So do I. So do I.'

The existence of the Rainbow was tied to her life, the power of the original families tied to her life. Surely, there was a backwards connection too. If she were to die, it would take decades or more before the full repercussions would be felt. But the repercussions would be felt. Her death would shatter the collective power of the Rainbow; her link to them would destroy them. Perhaps she could use that connection to send them message, to prepare them for the worst.

At the very least, she should be able to reach the Goldenrods of House Yellow. Charlotte Goldenrod could be trusted to inform the others without alerting anyone who might be in cahoots with Kayneth Kor or Joseph Moon.

Joseph Moon . . . The tentative musings of a slight smile played about her lips while her brows knitted together. There was something about that name . . . something she could potentially use, something useful, very useful – if she was right.

Contacting the Goldenrods would have to come first. House Yellow governed communication throughout the Rainbow, so theoretically, it shouldn't have been that hard to get them a message. But she was chained again, imprisoned again, and there was no way of knowing whether a message she sent would be intercepted.

Royce probably had ways of intercepting whatever messages she sent. Jibrayne would certainly be on the lookout for any of her potential correspondents. News of her escape from Trepidation would have reached even the deafest of ears by now.

Yarra slipped from the cuffs and placed them lightly on the ground. She sat cross-legged next to them, resting her chin on a fist, twisting absently at her bracelets. She could summon an air spirit, send it to House Yellow's base of operations, the Sky Tower. But would any spirit answer her call when they had all avoided her before and avoided Erryk, who had been sent to seek them out? It had to be worth a try though, right?

Yarra decided to give it a go. She had nothing to lose. Air spirits could get in and out of anywhere easily, so she had no need to worry about sneaking the spirit in. The only problem lay in getting one to answer her at all. And if one did respond, the next challenge would be getting it to listen.

'To the ancient skies above, I pray,' she began chanting. 'To the winds and clouds, hear what I say.'

It didn't have to rhyme, but she enjoyed the challenge. Whenever she could, she made sure to go out of her way to make understanding anything she said unnecessarily difficult. Such was her right. Besides, it was fun.

'Hear my call but do take heed. To hoard information is to indulge in greed. Carry my message swift and true to those rare and gifted few. The fate of the world is at stake. Please, please help me change this wretched fate.'

She waited, eyes closed, hands resting lightly on her crossed knees, searching with every facet of her very extensive magic, straining against the repulsive touch of her bracelets.

It was the slight lifting of her midnight hair in the stale, still air of her cell that alerted her to the presence of the spirit, the only one to have answered her call.

'The chosen few?' it asked in a lilting voice laced heavily with concealed laughter. The spirit remained invisible, but Yarra knew it was hovering above her head.

'Those aside from myself who have the aptitude and skill to summon a spirit such as yourself.'

'I know who you mean,' the spirit snapped. 'They are good people who do not deserve to be dragged into whatever world-threatening plot you clearly want them involved in.'

Yarra almost smiled. 'They are already involved. I just want to make sure they survive. Will you help?'

The spirit agreed and flittered away, carrying what Yarra hoped would be a life-saving message. Charlotte Goldenrod and her family had their own ways of getting messages to the other original families. The survivors, however precious few there may be left, needed to know what was about to happen. They needed to be prepared. So did she.

Joseph Moon had given her an idea. Her extensive knowledge of the Rainbow and the Amaryllis family only strengthened the belief she had in her fledgling theory. Nifilious would be able to confirm it. Once he did, the hard bit would really start.

She slipped out of the cell cloaked in shadows. Zenon never suspected a thing. Let him report to Royce that she was still chained and contained within. Let him play the loyal traitor. So she left in silence, slipped through the corridors in shadow, stealthily and sneakily avoiding the guards and Mossmans. Even Royce didn't notice her as he hurried past, toting a pile of books the ancient god had no doubt bestowed on him moments before.

'I want to know how good the spies were at disappearing into the dark they controlled,' she demanded of the creature, striding into the labyrinth of books unafraid.

'Looking to resurrect them, are we?'

'I just need to know if there are any left to carry on the bloodline. Any at all, no matter how far removed or how weak the magic they carry. Just if there are any left, no matter how far removed or how unaware they might be of the truth.'

'What would you give for such information?' Nifilious asked slyly, grinning through the dark.

Yarra stilled. 'I would give an arm and a leg. I would give my life if I thought that would make you change your mind. What do you want?' Suspicion laced her words.

'Royce is planning a takeover,' the ancient creature drawled, 'a very hostile takeover, by the sound of it. The vampires are planning a war. Your old friend plots to destroy you.'

Yarra didn't ask how he knew; he wouldn't tell her, not for free.

'And now you, it seems, are plotting something as well. What is it? I wonder.'

'Wouldn't you like to know?'

'I would, actually.'

'Hmmm.' Yarra smirked. She saw where this was headed now, where it had always been headed since the very beginning. 'I'd be willing to tell you . . . perhaps. If . . .' Another smirk.

'If I tell you about the surviving Amaryllis descendants.'

Yarra's grey eyes lit up in triumph. 'So there are surviving members.'

The darkness that was Nifilious seemed to swirl and writhe with anger and frustration. 'You . . . you tricked me,' he growled, seething.

'You make it too easy,' Yarra quipped back, grinning.

'So a few of them still live. So what?' If Nifilious had corporeal hands, Yarra imagined he would have thrown them up in the air. 'You don't know where they are. You have no way of finding them.'

'As long as I know they're out there, I can find them. You forget who I am, what I can do. How even the stars and the moon would bow to me if I asked. How do you know they're out there anyway?'

Nifilious's grin was a palpable thing, as evil and malicious as any demon's. 'They were spies, the best of the best, with sources everywhere and access to everything. There was no way a family as skilled as them was hunted to extinction. Think about it. Really think. I'm sure you have already. The best spies know how to disappear. And disappear, they did. Without a trace. The bubbliest and brightest of red-headed souls bathed in blessings of darkness and shadows faded completely from the world.'

'But redheads remain, families passing on the gene on from generation to generation. Families carrying names associated with that darkness. Names but none of the power.' Yarra's eyes shone like miniature stars in the stifling darkness Nifilious bought. She spoke just to antagonise him further. All this, she had already surmised.

'Exactly,' Nifilious said. 'Now tell me what you have planned.'

The grin Yarra gave the rumbling dark was pure wolf. 'No.'

The very foundations of the library seemed to shake.

'But,' she said as the rumbling grew and she began to fear that Nifilious might actually break something, 'you're most welcome to come watch.'

The growling stopped in an instant. Nifilious was never allowed out of the library. This place was his prison as much as the pledge was hers.

'I will give you permission to temporarily leave this place and observe. Observe. Nothing more and only for a short time.' Yarra watched the impenetrable dark closely, looking for any sign. 'At the coming convergence, you have permission to attend. I hope you find it enjoyable.'

Laughter lightly brushed past her face, as soft and gentle as a lover's kiss. 'If I were you, little she-devil, I'd worry less about the family you've yet to find and more about the family you struggle so desperately to keep.'

It was as good a thank you as she'd ever get, gratitude shown in the only way the ancient, bitter creature knew how, a warning for her about the people she loved, a warning she would not waste, even if she didn't understand it fully.

23

Truths

Yarra found Ray, Kelly, and Matt in the war room, standing around Erryk's large map and the pieces placed atop it. Zenon stood mute by the door, ever the loyal guard. Someone else must be guarding her cell. The Mossmans looked up as she entered. She grinned at them.

'Does he know?' Ray asked, sounding almost bitter.

She nodded.

'So now both he and Jibrayne know of the pledge. What are the chances that both of them would learn of the Rainbow's best-kept secret and both would plot to end us all?'

'Rather low, I imagine,' Kelly said. 'Who's Jibrayne?'

The way Kelly held herself was enough to make you forget the disfigurement done to her. She held herself with such confidence, such poise that there was no way one could see her as anything but perfect. Her golden mahogany hair had always framed her face like a halo; now it shone even brighter.

'A vampire we met when we were kids,' Ray said, indicating himself and Yarra.

'Is Royce really going to have us replaced?' Matt asked quietly.

'As surely as the sky is blue and the grass green, the cuckoo will take over the nest,' Yarra said.

All three Mossmans levelled her with a look. She rolled her eyes, fiddling with her bracelets.

'Does he have enough to convince them?' Kelly asked.

'With the pledge, no doubt,' Ray said.

'What else does he have?'

Ray let out a long sigh. He watched Yarra for a moment, a slight frown creasing his brow as she bent over the large map and began prodding the figures with a slim finger.

'Royce has all the soldiers and guards on his side,' Ray said. 'He will say that since he was able to sway them so easily, it reflects poorly on me. He will say that the soldiers must have had no respect for me if they listened to him so easily.'

'Zenon, is this true?' Matt asked.

The soldier nodded solemnly.

'Royce believes Zenon is on his side,' Ray continued. 'He believes that to have turned Zenon to his side is the ultimate proof of his victory. He will tell the convergence that if Zenon could be turned, if his loyalty to me and House Green was so easily swayed, then I am unfit to be lord.'

'The Beryls were removed by majority vote,' Kelly said slowly. 'There is no way, no way in all the hells that the leaders will not use that to call another vote to get rid of you.' She gaped up at her brother, devastation etched deep across her scarred face.

'Where will we go?' Matt asked softly, clutching tightly to Kelly's arm, his fingers digging into her skin, leaving half-moon marks on the patchwork of scars. 'They can't force us out of our home.'

'They can,' Yarra said without looking up from the map. 'Izrabella Dijon would have been left on the streets had her healing ability not been so valuable.'

'We can fight them,' Kelly said fiercely.

Ray shook his head. 'We would lose. Once we are gone, they will move to replace the Oxbloods and the Goldenrods. Then the Rainbow will be no more. There would be nothing to stop the monsters taking over our world. Jibrayne will attack, and all will be lost.'

The Mossman siblings all hung their heads. The twins bowed their heads together, Kelly's golden hair and Matt's creamier locks blending together. Ray stood apart, well aware he had caused this and was powerless to do anything to fix it. Zenon watched them in silence, as saddened as they were.

'How do we know this Jibrayne person is even behind the war?' Kelly asked. 'For all we know, it could be the demon kings themselves.'

'It's her, all right,' Yarra said with a small laugh.

She waved at Zenon, calling him over. He and the Mossmans crowded around the map as Yarra continued to laugh darkly.

'Oh, it's most definitely her,' Yarra said, snapping her fingers.

Instantly, the green and black markers representing the monster armies slid across the map into their real-life positions. As Yarra did this, her slate-grey eyes glowed a faint silver. Steam curled from under her bracelets.

'Look,' she said, pointing to a green marker just outside the border of the Violet Lands. 'These are werewolf troops but rogues.' She shook her head. 'Even if Nerys has disappeared, there is no way the other elders would allow such a force to present itself so close to our lands. To any of our lands.'

'They attacked us in our own home,' Kelly reminded her, sneering a little.

'Yes, but there was a mix of breeds,' Yarra said still not looking up from the map. 'The ones with poison on their talons usually stalk heights of the Maalia Mountains. They are the scourge of the Trepidation guards. The other packs make a point of not associating with them.'

Yarra pointed to another point on the map, this time a cluster of green and black markers deep in the heart of the Wild Lands.

'This shouldn't be here,' Yarra said, eyes still softly glowing. 'Vampires and werewolves together, so close, they could touch, yet they are not fighting. And here.' Yarra pointed to the border of the Green and Yellow Lands, to the place where the Maalia Mountains rolled into hills and the Ashdown Forest thinned into sparse clusters of trees. 'There should not be vampires here, not so deep into our space.'

Ray frowned. 'They are almost on the Green Lands, yet I have not felt them. If they are not here, they must be in the Yellow Lands, but Charlotte is even more in tune with her lands than I am.'

'They are there. I'm sure of it.'

Ray didn't dare tell her otherwise. He had told Royce Yarra was a seer, but she hardly ever used that power, the rules she lived by far more effective than the power she'd been blessed with. But now . . . her eyes glowed with a silver light unique only to her.

'Zenon, would the base of the Maalia Mountains provide enough cover to hide a small army?'

The old soldier shook his head. 'The Beryls know the Cerulean Gardens better than any other parts of their lands.'

Yarra nodded. 'But the Beryls are not monitoring the Blue Lands like they have done in the past. Relieved of their lordship, they live in exile. Besides' – Yarra tapped the map over the area where the Maalia Mountains slipped into the Blue Lands and formed the westernmost edge of the Cerulean Gardens – 'they have somehow harnessed the ghosts' ability to hide.'

'That's impossible,' Kelly said.

'Erryk said the ghosts were missing from the Ghost Lands,' Ray said, recalling the last report he had received from his younger brother. 'The banshees too were missing.'

'Why does this make you think Jibrayne is behind this?' Zenon asked.

Yarra just tapped a finger to the map, white light flashing from her fingertip.

Zenon and the Mossmans leaned forward and then recoiled as one. Hidden deep in the Ashdown Forest, firmly in the Green Lands, where the ruins of the old kings' castle once stood, Yarra's magic revealed two black pieces transformed. Both pieces were now pink; both had smiling faces and fangs dripping blood. The transformed pieces held a banner between them, its edges flapping in a phantom wind.

'"We wait here,"' Kelly read out. 'What does that mean?'

Yarra blinked, and her eyes returned to their normal blank and disinterested grey, although she swayed slightly and leaned heavily on the table for support. 'We're about to find out.'

A ghost materialised before them, standing in the middle of the table, everything below the waist obscured by the map. He was old. Even as he was a ghost, that was obvious.

'Romney,' Yarra said by way of greeting her head in her hands as she fought the aftereffects of her magic.

The wizened ghost inclined his head and spread his arms wide. In each of his translucent hands, he held a piece of delicate pink paper. Ray took one, Kelly the other. They read them, and their faces fell.

'What?' Yarra asked. 'What?'

Two papers came her way. Zenon leaned over her shoulder to read it.

'*What is this?*' Ray demanded, reaching out to grab Romney, but his hands went straight through him.

The ancient ghost smiled sadly and vanished.

Ray rounded on Yarra, malice dripping from him. 'You are not coming.'

'I am,' Yarra said quietly, too quietly.

'You. Are. Not,' he said. 'Zenon, take her back to her room and lock her in. Make sure there is no way she can escape.'

Zenon nodded once, and Yarra was dragged out of the war room, screaming.

'Find Annika. Tell her what's happened.'

The twins' faces paled slightly, but Kelly and Matt nodded. Ray's gaze was one of pure rage, his eyes like emerald fires.

'House Green is at war.'

24

Action

Royce carried the books back to his room with the same level of care one might carry a very large, very expensive diamond crystal vase – or a child, he supposed; children were precious too. Nifilious had handed them over easily enough after Annika had left. The mysterious creature had piled up book after book and given him a brief one-sentence and sometimes one-word summary of their contents.

In the end, he had left with only two volumes. The first was old, really old, titled, *Dawn till Dusk*. The cover was so worn and aged, Nifilious had insisted he keep it wrapped in a cloth to prevent any further damage and threatened to eat him whole if he returned it in any worse a condition than it was in now. Royce hadn't seen Nifilious's body, didn't even know if the creature had a mouth; nevertheless, he had no doubt the creature could and would eat him and resolved to wear gloves and use extreme caution when reading that particular book. Nifilious had told him it was basically an encyclopaedia of everything the White had done, who they were, and how they died.

'Dramatised memoirs' had been Nifilious's exact words.

The second book he had taken with him, he felt slightly guilty about reading, for in fact, it was not a book at all but a diary or journal logging the thoughts and feelings of one Yarra White. Royce had only flipped through a few pages, but he knew the words hidden in those pages could very well reveal the deepest, darkest, innermost workings of her mind. It was like peering into her soul, something he was curious to see – if only to confirm she had one – but not entirely comfortable doing.

'If Yarra had not wanted you to read it,' Nifilious said, 'she would not have left it where you could find it.'

And that had been that. He carried his treasures through the halls towards his room near the guards' barracks. He would have ample time to read later. Reading and planning often went hand in hand, and now that he knew of the pledge, he could overthrow not only the Mossmans but possibly the Oxbloods too. The Goldenrods would be tricky, but if he got the council on his side, if the leaders of the other houses saw, as he did, the dangers of having leaders pledged to give their lives for a single reckless individual . . .

Yes, it was possible, a complete restructure of the Rainbow, a council unlike there had ever been before, with houses run by people who deserved respect and were worthy to rule rather than a title passed through families that weren't needed or were unstable or inadequate.

But they had good reason for pledging themselves to her. The Rainbow had been built of the backbone of the founders' magic. Their descendants, the originals, had that same power. He did not want to cripple the Rainbow. He wanted to make it stronger. Over the years, the original families had weakened. It didn't matter that their power remained essential to their continued triumph over the monsters. If they were too weak to rule, as the Mossmans were, they needed to be replaced, simple as that.

He marched through the halls, oblivious to the growing chaos around him, a grin spreading over his face. Once he revealed the pledge to the other houses, he was bound to get them on his side. Kayneth Kor and Joseph Moon were bound to support his bid for power in House Green. Dean and Lynda Couvrette too were more likely to back him than not.

He reached his room and closed the door behind him smiling. As shouts from outside increased and voices drew ever closer, barking questions and demands, Royce placed the books on the corner of his desk and drew a large sheet of paper towards him.

Yes, he thought, *this could work. This might actually work.*

Quickly, he sketched a list of all the things he needed, all the points he needed to get the leaders of the other houses to back his bid for power, all the points he had gathered about Ray Mossman and House Green, about the pledge and the perilous position it would leave the Rainbow in should Yarra meet an unfortunate and untimely end. Then he went back, filled in the blanks, took creative liberties to explain the vaguer points, outright lied about others.

He gazed down at his masterpiece, the pinnacle of all those decades building and fostering trust, the bones of a plan that would grow to be an unstoppable monster, a beast to tear down the current order and rebuild a stronger one in his image.

Now came the hard part: filling in the details and hammering out the finer points so that nothing could go wrong, so that he had contingencies for every possibility, so that there was no chance for surprises to catch him off guard.

But was it right?

To reveal the pledge would mark Yarra as a target. He held no love for the spitfire assassin, but even he was not stupid enough not to recognise the reason the pledge existed in the first place.

He had been right when he had told Ray he thought the girl was key to winning this war. He had been right to think that if she used her power, they would win.

If he revealed the pledge, if he revealed the secret kept by so few . . . yes, he could sway the council to his side, spur the way forward for a stronger Rainbow. But he could doom them too.

They would target her for her extraordinary magic. The assassin would become a target. The secrecy that had kept her and her family safe for generations would no longer exist. And with her protectors so few . . .

She would die. She would be killed for that miraculous magic she possessed. They would kill her to prevent her using her limitless magic power against them. And he could not allow that to happen. He could not allow her life to be snuffed.

It didn't matter if her magic was truly a thing to be feared. Because if she died, magic died too.

She wasn't just Yarra White, last of her family line and leader of the Rainbow, possible the only seer in existence and the most feared assassin in all of Verstra. She wasn't just a criminal or a thief. She *was* magic.

The door to his room banged open. Royce started so suddenly, he upset a glass of water, the liquid surging for the ancient tome perched precariously on the edge of the desk.

'Sir!' the soldier gasped, saluting sharply.

Royce grabbed the book, smoothing the cloth cover and hoping Nifilious wouldn't be able to detect any damage when he returned the book.

'What is it?' he snapped.

'Sir, we have a problem,' the soldier said.

'What sort of problem?'

'It's the Mossmans, sir.'

'Report,' Royce commanded.

'Lord Ray has declared war, sir,' the soldier said.

Royce considered the soldier. Before Royce had been appointed captain of the guard and set about changing things from within, the soldier had been one of Ray's closest confidantes, not as close as Zenon had been. To have turned such a soldier was proof of his superiority and another point to add to his list. If he could inspire loyalty in guards who had served House Green for centuries, he was clearly the best choice for leader, better than Ray at least, Ray, who had lost the loyalty of the men he had turned, men like Zenon and the soldier before him.

Royce felt himself pale. 'Explain.'

'It appears Master Erryk has gone missing, sir,' the soldier said.

'That is hardly a reason for war, soldier.'

'Agreed, sir, but Lord Ray appears to believe that the vampires are behind his disappearance and has declared war to bring him back.'

'Foolish child! Does he think to intimidate them in to giving up?'

'It is possible, sir. I cannot speak to the lord's mind.'

Royce smiled ruefully. 'What evidence does Ray claim to have proving that it is indeed the vampires behind this?' he asked.

'Reports are that the wards are still down from the werewolf attack,' the soldier said, 'and that when he went in search of Master Erryk's latest report, Lord Ray found the window of the aviary torn off its hinges. Several of the guards also reported seeing large shapes fly overhead, larger than our own pigeons, but they say they were distracted and so thought nothing of it.'

He'd have to have a word with those guards, make sure they were paying attention at all times and not distracted by anything while on shift. Still . . .

'That's hardly sufficient evidence to go to war.'

The soldier nodded. 'Agreed, sir. That's why I came to find you, to put a stop to this. They are in the armoury, sir.'

Royce nodded grimly, setting his jaw. 'And the girl?' he asked as an afterthought as he strode through his door. 'What of her?'

'Ms White?' the soldier asked.

Royce nodded.

'She said that as her fight with you, sir, resulted in getting her throat slit and almost dying, the victory was yours. She consented to being chained and is currently locked back in her cell.'

Royce spared one stunned second to blink.

'Congratulations on your victory, sir,' he said, admiration gleaming in his eyes.

'I didn't do anything,' Royce said, frowning at her motives. 'She slit her own throat.'

He left the stunned soldier in his room and hurried to the armoury, barking orders to every soldier and guard he passed to stand down and to sure up the library's defences and to not make ready to attack.

When he finally reached the armoury, he feared he was too late, too late to make a show of trying to stop them, to look like the distressed but loyal captain of the guard trying to stop his lord doing something foolish. Of course, if all the Mossmans went off to war with the vampires and none of them returned, it would make his life a whole lot easier, but he had to at least appear like he was concerned.

The Mossmans were prepared for war.

Ray had donned his ceremonial green cloak, the hilt of his great sword gleaming from over his shoulder. He wore light armour, and his emerald eyes seemed to burn with rage.

Kelly had her golden hair tied back. It revealed the true extent of her new scar, an angry red line ripping from the side of her mouth up her cheek to her ear. She wore tight-fitting pants and a singlet top, with daggers strapped in two bandoliers crossed over her chest. Even though gauntlets covered her forearms, the scars of what the werewolves had done to her were clearly visible. Yet she wore them with pride, smiled in such a way that that scar, that horrible scar, seemed almost to disappear. That was until she turned to face him, and Royce saw that same murderous glint in her eyes. Now her smile looked like one of a demon. That scar exemplifying the vicious hard flash of teeth.

Matt stood statue still by his twin, almost back to back, the silent, deadly shadow to her golden ray of death.

Annika had changed into her war dress. As frilly and as pink as all her other favourite clothes, this one, he knew, was different. The bodice was armoured and the skirts lined with the thinnest of metal sheets. Should a monster or vampire encounter her frilly skirts, they would soon find themselves sliced to pieces. Her twin rapiers were sheathed at her hips, their handles disguised by the bows adorning her waist and wrists.

'What is the meaning of this?' he asked abruptly and without waiting for an invitation.

'Ready your men,' Ray replied. 'We storm the vampire coven as soon as you are able.'

'Why?'

Ray rounded on him in an instant. 'You have no right to question me! Ready the men for battle at once!'

Royce stood his ground. 'No,' he said, short, sharp, and simple.

Ray glared at him, rage simmering just below the surface, but again, he spooled it back in. reeled himself back from the brink of anger-induced rage. 'We are at war,' he said tersely. 'Ready the men for immediate attack.'

'We're at war?' Royce asked. 'Since when?'

'Since those bastard vampires kidnapped our brother!' Annika said.

'Surely, Erryk is simply searching for one of the girl's wayward friends,' Royce said, praying he lived through this despite the line he was toeing here. 'Perhaps he is still within the Ghost Lands and you have just failed to locate him. You have searched, haven't you? You're not just jumping to unnecessary conclusions?'

'We searched,' Ray said tightly, lips pursed. 'We searched everywhere. They took him. They have him.'

'Where is your evidence? Your proof?'

Royce didn't know where such boldness was coming from. Perhaps it came from the confidence he had in his fledgling plan to overthrow him, perhaps the knowledge that going to war was a terrible idea and that he knew he had to stop them by any means necessary – or at least appear to want to stop them.

'*Proof?*' Annika shrieked. 'We don't need proof. They could be hurting him right now. We have to go!'

Mutely, Matt handed him a note. Royce scanned it quickly, frowning.

We're coming for you . . .
There's nothing you can do
Try as you might
You won't win this fight

Vampires are smart
Vampires are strong
Jibrayne said you were all stupid
She was right all along

Lola, Lola is the best
Bite the head off all the rest

'What is this?' he asked.

Kelly handed him a similar note, written on the same pink paper, flowers around the border and a similar curling, almost illegible female script.

House Green, it has been seen
To taste the very best

Lola dear can have this one
Lorelai will eat the rest

So much bloodshed there will be
A feast they'll be for Lola dear and me

'And this proves what exactly?'

'This proves the vampires have Erryk,' Kelly said. 'We need to leave. Now.'

'So this Lola and Lorelai are vampires. So what? This does not give you sufficient cause to declare war.'

'It is reason enough,' Ray said. 'Lola and Lorelai are known conspirators of Jibrayne, a vampire we know to be plotting against the Rainbow. Her name is even mentioned in the second note. We are going to rescue Erryk. There's nothing you can do to stop us. Take it to the convergence if you like. Use this in your argument to overthrow me. I don't care. We're going.'

Ray finished the last of his preparations and nodded to his siblings. The four of them levelled dangerously gleaming emerald eyes his way.

'You can come if you like,' Kelly offered. 'We could use your help.'

Royce shook his head, slightly aghast. Then the four of them strode from the room, armed to the teeth and ready to rage war on those who dared pry their family apart.

One thing kept Royce rooted to the spot, one thing he couldn't shake, one thing that bugged him. Ray knew he was plotting to overthrow him, had probably guessed that the wealth of knowledge he had accumulated afforded him a fair shot at winning over the other leaders. Ray probably knew that the only support he would get at such a council would come from House Red and House Yellow, the only houses that continued to be led by their traditional families. Ray knew this and still allowed Royce to be captain of the guard, allowed him access to family secrets, even gave him more fuel to add to the fire. It was strange – helpful but strange.

'Send messages to all the houses!' he barked as he too swept from the armoury. 'I want all the lords and leaders to convene as soon as possible.'

'You're calling a convergence?' a soldier asked, pausing mid-step for clarification. 'What for?'

'I'm calling a convergence to discuss the removal of Ray Mossman from his position of power within House Green and present myself as suitable replacement.'

He was almost sure to succeed now, especially if all the Mossmans got themselves killed in their stupid war against the vampires.

With any luck, Erryk would be dead already – or worse.

25

Search

R ay knew he shouldn't go, that he should stay and stop Royce from staging his ridiculous coup. But Erryk . . . He couldn't lose his brother, not now, not ever. Even if saving him meant losing leadership of House Green and destroying the family he had tried so hard to keep together over the years . . . then so be it.

He knew that Royce had a point. He had no real evidence pointing to the vampires as the culprits. The notes could have been nothing more than threats. Gods knew he had received more than his fair share of those. Alone, he might not have considered them at all, but Yarra had reacted in a way she rarely did, and whatever her faults, numerous though they may be, she was never wrong, not about family, not when she actually used her magic.

Although how she had managed that small feat with her magic stifled by those Rowan ash and iron bracelets was another matter entirely.

'How are we going to find him?' Annika asked.

'We already know where he is,' Ray said, 'the border between our lands and the Yellow Lands. That castle Yarra showed us, remember?'

'Yes,' Kelly said, 'but you can't sense them, can you? How do we know they're even really there?'

'They're there,' Matt said quietly.

Kelly turned to her twin, emerald eyes softening. Matt seemed oblivious; he just stared at Ray.

'Yarra,' Matt said, 'right? She used her power, not the shadows or whatever other magics she uses whenever she feels like it but her real power. The magic only she has. As the last White.'

Ray nodded. 'Yarra is a seer. It's why she talks in riddles, partly because she thinks it's funny, partly because it adds a layer of mystery to her, but mostly because she sees the truth. All of it. And only riddles are safe enough to share with the rest of us.'

'I think she just likes it,' Annika said.

Kelly and Matt nodded.

Ray smiled grimly. 'So we know the vampires are definitely there. And that they have Erryk.'

'So how are we going to get there?' Kelly asked, rephrasing her original question.

'They're still within the Green Lands, right?' Annika asked. 'Can't we jump there?'

Anyone with strong enough magic could jump. It was the relatively simple trick of moving oneself from one place to another. Usually, one could only jump about a hundred metres, but within the Green Lands, anyone with elemental earth magic had their magic amplified. The same was true for the other lands too. The Mossmans could jump to any point within their lands, Ray, as lord, could jump further.

'We could be jumping into a trap,' Ray said. 'They could be expecting that.'

'But what choice do we have? We have to save Erryk.'

'Are we really going to do this,' Matt asked, 'leave Royce to destroy us?'

'Don't worry,' Kelly said. 'We'll be home soon enough.'

'We might not have a home to come back to, you know,' Matt said quietly, meeting the eyes of his siblings with an unflinching gaze.

Ray sighed. 'I know.'

'What about Yarra?' Kelly asked.

'Zenon took her back to her cell,' Annika said. 'He probably spelled the chains too. She should be safe.'

Kelly shook her head. Matt smiled ruefully.

Ray let loose a long sigh. 'Now we'll have to save her too, I suppose.'

'What do you mean?' Annika asked. 'She wouldn't go and try rescue Erryk on her own, would she?'

Kelly levelled her sister with a look of stunned disbelief and blank shock. 'This is Yarra we're talking about. Of course, she would.'

'But . . . he spelled her in, wrapped her in iron and Rowan ash. Even she could not get out of that.'

Kelly just smiled. 'Go see for yourself if you don't believe us.'

Annika stared at her siblings, at the brothers and sister who gave her equal small knowing smiles and watched as she stalked from the room and returned moments later, fluttering a tattered slip of paper between her fingers.

'What's it say?' Ray asked, a slight mocking chuckle in his voice.

Sighing, Annika read, 'Rule Seven.'

Ray clapped his hands. 'So now we have to save her too. Great. Just great.'

'What's Rule Seven?' Annika asked.

'Of all the rules Yarra lives by, Rule Seven was made just for us. For those who pledge to protect her. To let us know she is planning to do something stupid,' Matt said.

'A plan that will require us to save her,' Kelly continued, 'else we risk losing her forever.'

Ray met his sister's eyes, Annika held firm. He held out his hands. Matt took his left, Kelly his right, the circle complete as Annika grasped hands with her siblings. Ray took a moment to meet each of their eyes.

'Ready?' he asked – and jumped.

26

Chase

Yarra tracked blind. It was not a visible trace she was following, nor was it a scent. What she followed was more of a sixth sense, a feeling. Others had described it as magic – others thought it was magic – but the truth was she didn't know what it was. She just knew that there was an invisible thread that would lead her to her target and that if she followed it, regardless of where it led, she would find Erryk.

It was her magic that warned her to run faster.

So she ran, leaves and stones churned up in her wake. She vaulted over a fallen tree, scraping her palm over the bark but not pausing or flinching in the slightest. Although she ran blind, she did not falter or worry about collisions with the trees, her sixth sense alerting her to anything that might impede her speed.

She slowed momentarily. Ahead of her was a cliff. Climbing it would take time. Blind as she was, it would also be cumbersome and hard. Her moment of indecision was followed by a flash of subtle darkness as she slipped into shadow and re-emerged atop the cliff, feet flying beneath her as that thread pulled tighter.

It was not hard to understand why she was feared, why her power was legend unto itself. She was still wearing her Rowan ash and iron bracelets, her magic stifled and blocked from her reach. But she slipped through shadows as easily as breathing, moved trees and living obstacles of the Ashdown Forest subtly out of her way as she fled past.

She ran on and on, jumping through the darkness whenever obstacles required more than a second to overcome. She knew Ray would be mad at her for leaving, knew that the soldiers thought her chained and secured in her cell. They had even spelled the room, warded it against her escape with iron and Rowan ash to nullify her magic. But she didn't need magic to break out of the Ivy Library, not when she knew every nook and cranny of the place. She was Yarra White, notorious assassin, and no chains had ever held her, not for long.

Myrthos adorned her head like a gleaming crown of death, its wicked barbs like stars against her night-black hair. An equally bright gleam in her eyes and reflected off the flash of teeth: that was the last thing those vampire sentries saw as she stabbed her daggers into their chests.

How long would it be before Lola and Lorelai realised she was here?

Their hideout was more of a fortress. It was literally a huge castle, old and fortified, as all good castles were. It was also painted black, which, Yarra supposed, showed considerable restraint, knowing the vampire sisters' tendency towards fluoroes. There was even a moat – sprinkled with glitter. Well, so much for that.

The sentries she had just taken out without so much as blinking had been stationed at the foremost gates, between the first two pillars of fortified and menacing-looking bars. The next wave of guards were inside the moat. Yarra flashed her teeth at them from afar.

Seconds later, she was behind them, daggers flashing. They were undead, immortal and faster, but she had surprise on her side, and for the first one, that was all she needed. She sliced her dagger through the back of his neck, his unearthly dying screech a song in her ears.

Even Lola and Lorelai couldn't overlook such an obvious sign as that.

She twisted and threw her second dagger, sparing no more than a brief glance to see it strike the second vampire in the chest before her attention was drawn to the rest, two more vampire sentries yet to be dealt with before she could enter the catacombs of the castle in search of Erryk.

The vampires snarled, fangs flashing and gleaming in the castle's torch light. She ducked under the clawing hands of one, only for the other to appear in her blind spot, fangs bared and daggers like claws on his hands. Her own daggers clashed against them, fast but not fast enough to avoid getting cut along her right bicep.

She snarled back at the vampire, kicking the one that had cut her and pouncing on the other, dagger angled down. The vampire's superior speed allowed him to avoid her, but she rolled, her dagger curving in a silver arc across the vampire's leg and then into his gut, opening him like a fish.

She left him there, bleeding in a pile of his own insides, and turned flashing teeth to the last. He snarled, licking his lips in an involuntary reaction to all the blood, and charged at her. Yarra waited, flipped over where she expected his attack to connect, and slammed her fist into his back. He lurched forward, and she lashed out with her legs.

The vampire stumbled, and she pounced. Slashing forward with her dagger, she drove the monster back. The vampire snarled and sprang forward. Superior speed and strength propelled him forward with great accuracy. In an instant, Yarra was pinned, her dagger twisted from her grip and the vampire's fangs dangerously close to her neck.

So Yarra simply dropped. She went limp, dropping in the vampire's grip so suddenly, he was pulled forward by her momentum. Her sudden drop was followed by a roll, a roll which pulled the vampire with her until he was flipped over her curling back and off the edge of the moat to fall flailing into the abyss of water below.

The stunt earned her another scratch, this one along her neck and across the back of her shoulder blade, but the vampires were dealt with, and Erryk still awaited his rescue. She yanked her dagger from the chest of the dead vampire and gripped its hilt firmly. She had work to do.

The thread pulled her deeper into the castle, into the belly of the beast where more of the bloodthirsty vampires lurked and waited for her to walk into their trap.

She walked carefully but quickly, wary of the traps she knew would be waiting for her. Lola and Lorelai had never been very discreet, so when she encountered the first trap, a tripwire that brought down a giant swinging axe from the roof, she was not surprised. The very obvious glittery pink tripwire was easy to avoid. She stepped over it with exaggerated caution, knowing the sisters were probably watching her, and ducked into a roll as the glittery silver axe swung free and sliced through the air towards her – triggered by a secondary device in the floor.

'You'll have to do better than that, Lola!' she called into the tunnels.

The shadows seemed to chuckle at that. Yarra took that as a sign she was getting closer or was at least heading in the right direction. Another trap, a false step outlined in fluorescent green – easily and quickly avoided. She continued on her way.

Shaking her head, she muttered, 'Much better than that.'

Unfortunately for her, it seemed that the sisters had improved their trap making in the century or so since she had last fought them. The next trap Yarra encountered, she fell for, hook, line, and sinker. She stepped over a second tripwire, this one shimmery blue, and fell straight through the floor.

She threw out her power, only to have it sucked into the vampire's original creation of magic-nullifying Rowan ash and iron hail that fell from a hidden chamber in the roof, cascading down on her like an unrelenting torrent of abuse. So she fell unaided and landed hard with an echoing and painful thump inside a tight circle of snarling vampires, each heavily armed with malice dripping from their swords, eyes, and fangs.

From the mass of snarling monsters, two figures emerged, dragging a third between them. The girl on the left had hair that fell well past her waist, dyed a vibrant, almost neon pink. Pink lipstick was smudged across her mouth and smeared on her gleaming long fangs. The girl on the right had equally long hair, dyed neon blue, and more precisely applied blue shimmer lip gloss.

Between them, hanging lifelessly from his arms, was Erryk.

His slightly curly hair was mattered with dirt, his shirt coated with it and with blood. Yarra scanned him quickly – blood on his face, hands, neck but no bite marks, not that she could see.

Yarra sketched a bow before the sisters. 'Lola, Lorelai, so good to see you again. It's been too long. So nice of you to look after Erryk for me and to greet me yourselves. How have you been? Are you well? How's Jibrayne? Did you miss me?'

The pink-haired girl cackled, doubling over with the force of her laughs. 'We caught you!' she howled. 'We caught you, we caught you, we caught you! Ha-ah ha-ah-ah!'

She snatched Erryk away from her sister and shook him like a doll. His head lolled to the side, exposing his neck. The vampire mimed biting him, lowering her fangs over his neck.

'I knew using this one as bait would draw you out. I knew it, I knew it, I knew it. Didn't I tell you, Lorelai? Didn't I, didn't I?'

The blue-haired vampire nodded earnestly. 'You did, Lola. Very clever.'

'Can I eat him now, Lorelai, pleeeease?'

'The others will be coming for him soon. Why don't you wait? Then you can have more. Besides' – a gleam of fangs under neon-blue hair – 'we have Yarra now. Why don't we snack on her instead?'

Twin pairs of blood-red eyes swivelled towards her. Yarra felt a shiver climb down her spine and frost spread through her veins. Her fall had not been bad, but she had cracked a few ribs and possibly her wrist, most likely her ankle too. Rule One should have kept her alive. If all went according to plan, the vampire sisters should have taken her prisoner, delivered her to Jibrayne personally, or locked her up for questioning, but Lola and her sister, Lorelai, were probably the only two beings alive that particular rule didn't apply to.

They were, for lack of a better word, crazy.

She gripped her daggers tighter in her hands, flipping one into a reverse grip and bringing it up just in time as the first of the vampires attacked.

27

Horrors

Royce went straight for the books, not the generalised ones he'd read before, the ones the disembodied Nifilious had given him before, but the ones Yarra herself had directed him to read, the ones Nifilious had handed over only after being released from whatever pledge Yarra had bound it by, the ones so secret, they required an ancient death god to keep them safe.

He pulled on a pair of gloves and gingerly, so, so carefully, lifted the dusty old cover of *Dusk till Dawn*. The first few chapters were vague, like they had been filled in generations later by descendants who had only heard the most fanciful stories of their ancestors, stories they entered as fact purely because it helped fuel the rumours surrounding their family.

Dragons, most proud a species if ever there was one, have but one weakness, not for gold or jewels or any other physical commodity but for flattery. Flatter a dragon, and you can get away with almost anything. Anger or offend one at your own peril. Any sane person knows this to be true. It is astounding, therefore, to learn that there are those who steal from and insult these most powerful and dangerous of beasts and live to tell the tale. Boasting over roaring hearth-side flames of feats such as these is the favourite pastime of one Bon Ellis White, who, legend claims, challenged a dragon to a race. The dragon, being one of the proud magical beasts they are, who also happen to possess the ability of flight, challenged Bon to a race to the top of the highest mountain. Bon Ellis White beat the dragon and claimed possession of its hoard and mastery

*over its minor magics. Mastery of dragon magic is just the latest in the
long, never-ending list of skills acquired and perfected by the White.*

All the early stories were similar – legends of individuals who bested
dragons in magic, flight, speed, and strength, who outmanoeuvred hordes
of vampires to emerge from the battlefield alive and unscathed, tales of
girls who could see the future, manipulate it to their will, and of boys who
could summon stars in corporeal form – all no doubt made up to booster
their own self-confidence, all falsified to lend credibility to the legendary
power of the White.

One common theme ran throughout all of them: overwhelming and
unsurpassed power coupled with supernatural athletic ability, inhuman
stamina, and a seemingly complete inability to feel any fear. All the early
stories were filled with magic and adventures with no mention of the
Rainbow or any pledge to protect them.

It was very clear when the Rainbow sprung into existence. Tales of
magical adventures turned to tales of conquest over demons and darkness.
Then there were tales of hiding, of fleeing across continents and hiking up
the tallest of mountains to escape the darkness that sought to end them.

Royce concluded this must have been the time Yarra told him about,
when the Rainbow had almost been destroyed and the pledge had been
created to ensure no such tragedy happened ever again. Then the stories
became more personal, written in third person to make the author seem
more than he or she had been in life.

*Erika Snow, greatest of all the branch families, greater than any of the
White, trekked around the world by herself in record time. Her exploits
were impeded by the efforts of the Rainbow, who wanted to keep her locked
up and protected like a delicate flower, and countless monsters whom Erika
Snow, greatest of them all, went out of her way to infuriate and annoy.*

The deeper Royce delved into the musty fragile pages of *Dusk till
Dawn*, the clearer the picture became. The Whites were adventurous,
foolhardy, and all-powerful, and the Rainbow had pledged to protect them
from harm. In the old days, that would have been impossible. There was no
way to keep them safe. They were too wilful, too powerful – too deranged.

April White, her partner, and two young children died today
after the volcano they had been scouting as a possible holiday
retreat exploded underneath them. House Yellow, who had
been tasked with protecting them, were executed in accordance
with the pledge and a branch family elevated to lordship.

So the Goldenrods hadn't always ruled House Yellow? Interesting. But House Yellow had always been close, had always ruled together. Royce doubted the change in leadership all those years ago had made much difference in the long run or that bringing up this change in leadership, this past failure of House Yellow, would help him dethrone Ray Mossman.

Generations and generations of White family history were concealed within these pages. Slowly, slowly, another pattern became clear. They were being tamed, their numbers dwindling, the tales of grand adventures all but gone from the pages. The Rainbow was winning the fight to keep the Whites contained and isolated. Protection was easy if the protected never left their room. Nifilious had said something similar.

Then there was just one, one child to carry on the White family name. That child married an outsider and had one child of their own, one full-blooded member of the White that all seven families of the Rainbow had pledged to protect. It was genius, really. Thousands and thousands of years had won the Rainbow a tamed and confined White. Generations and generations later had them all protecting one individual. A job that had seemed impossible in the beginning, a job that had seen whole families slaughtered, was now as simple as keeping one child alive.

For seventy generations, the Rainbow had succeeded. They had kept the White safe and contained and completely hidden from the rest of the world. Verstra never knew the touch of the White. For seventy generations, the White was protected by the Rainbow and hidden from everyone and everything.

Then Yarra had been born.

Seven families tasked with the protection of one child – yet Yarra had managed to escape.

Royce set aside *Dusk till Dawn*. The last entry was nothing more than a hurried scribble. Stygian and Ebony White's name had been crossed out with vicious red ink. Underneath was a single line in the same red script, seven words that declared her intention to the world.

Yarra White will restore order and balance.

Yarra had killed her parents, Royce knew this already, but to see the anger she had towards the woman who had given her life displayed and emphasised on the page in angry red . . . What had caused her to go so far? What had broken her so completely that she had snapped and slaughtered her parents so brutally? The brutality didn't fit with her. It was too personal, too violent.

Trepidation hadn't broken her; weeks of training hadn't broken her. What could possibly have happened to make her sadistically slaughter the very people who had given her life? It didn't fit.

Royce pulled forward the diary, the hand-written scrawl that detailed her deepest, darkest feelings and thoughts, and felt nothing but cold.

Not all monsters have fangs.

Not all monsters have claws and teeth or howl at the moon or drink the blood of innocents. Sometimes they can live inside the person you love most in this world. Sometimes the monster can live with you, care for you, even love you before shedding its terrible skin and tearing you apart.

Over and over again.

Sometimes it's all you can do not to turn the blade, the blade that has killed so many monsters, monsters of all shapes and sizes that snarled and fought back with tooth and claw, on yourself. Plunge that cold hard steel into flesh that quivers from the mere thought of the monster coming at you again.

Sometimes there's nothing stopping you from just grabbing that blade and sliding it gently across your wrists or neck, allowing the sharpened edge to part skin like a hot knife through butter.

Sometimes the only thing stopping you from ending the miserable thing you call a life is a simple small fear. Not fear of the blood – god

*knows you've seen enough blood not to be squeamish at the sight
of it — nor fear of the pain. Pain is an old friend, there with you
always as you hunt those responsible, those monsters.*

*No, it's not the pain or the blood that stop you from
taking that one final fatal leap into nothingness. It's the
irritation that you know accompanies failure.*

*All those times you've tried, all those cuts you've made across
your skin scab and heal and itch. It's the itch that stops you. The
itch of healing skin, flesh that heals so much more easily than
the scarred remnants of what you struggle to call a soul.*

*Yet still you try. Still, you slice that blade across scarred wrists, watching as
blood wells to the surface, warming your skin and arms as it covers them.*

*No, it's not the monsters that scare you. All the werewolves, krakens,
and vampires you've faced over the years pale in comparison to the
monster you found in the one person you truly thought you loved.*

Not all monsters have fangs.

*The ones that do are easy to find, easy to fight. The ones that
don't hide in plain sight, they pretend to be normal, convince
you to trust them, and then tear your world apart.*

*As horrible as it seems, as horrible as it is, it is these monsters
that make the world work the way it does. As unfortunate
as such a revelation is, it doesn't change the facts.*

*Monsters live inside us. They are us, and we are them. It is the way
the world works. How it always has been and will always be.*

*Pity those who face us. Pity the werewolves and the vampires who stand
in our way, for the true monsters are the ones that live within us.*

Pity them. They don't have a chance.

Royce shut the book with shuddering hands. Such rage. Such hate. The fear and anger she must have felt, might still feel, was so tangible, so clear, it dripped from each letter, curled around every sentence and phrase. Her suffering washed over him in a wave, and he cringed.

But there was also sadness, such profound sadness, he couldn't help but feel a wave of grief and pity well up within him.

The last piece he needed to make his case to the remaining lords and convince the leaders to side with him – as much as he hated himself for using her sadness against her, as immoral as it was, he would win. He would crush her and the Mossmans and elevate himself to his rightful position as ruler.

He had ordered his subordinate to call a council meeting. Everyone would be there. This would be his one chance to present his case before them all. This was sink or swim for him. Years and years, he had worked on this takeover, fostering trust and sowing the seeds of dissent. It would all come down to this. He was more than ready. His contingency plans had contingency plans.

Learning what he had about the White and about Yarra had just been the icing on the cake of victory. He didn't bother to hide his grin as he strode through the Ivy Library, didn't bother to conceal his excitement or his feelings of triumph. His plans were complete, the traps set, the convergence called.

Everything was in place for his takeover. All that was left to do was present his piece to the other lords, to give the leaders of the other houses irrefutable proof that Ray Mossman was unfit to rule.

Ray had a spare ceremonial green cloak. Royce donned it. It made a statement, but so did everything he was about to do.

All Royce had left to do was win.

28

Premonitions

Ray's frown grew deeper and deeper the further they went, the further he and his siblings pushed their magic into the jump. They were still inside the Green Lands. He hadn't yet felt the drag on his power crossing the border caused.

Their destination was within the Green Lands too. They already knew that, but the confirmation was not comforting – which meant those vampires were hiding their presence, not just hiding their presence but also erasing it completely. He was second only to Charlotte Goldenrod when it came to sensing monsters inside his lands, and yet Erryk had been taken – by vampires, their hideout inside his lands, and he had had no idea.

'It's not your fault,' Matt said through hard breaths.

Ray said nothing, glowering.

Annika's battle dress flowed out behind her, trailing over sticks and leaves but never getting caught. 'Does Yarra know who did this?' she asked. 'Does she know why?'

'Jibrayne, I understand, I think,' Kelly panted, her injuries, although healed, troubling her still. 'The others, Lola and Lorelai, I don't know.'

'Who is Jibrayne again?' Annika asked.

Ray slowed slightly, licking his lips, tasting the words. All four of them were still moving, rushing through that between space as they jumped.

'When I was little,' he said, 'Yarra and her parents were living in the Ivy Library. Yarra understandably hated it. One day she broke out. Bear in mind, this was the time when Yarra and her parents were under strict guard. Yarra was confined to the suite of safety rooms built especially for her in the centre of the library and guarded around the clock. For her to have escaped should have been impossible.'

'But she got out anyway,' Annika said, voice full of admiration.

Ray nodded. 'She got out. First thing she does is let Achilles out of the grounds to play. Her demon hound is perhaps the most loyal creature you'll ever meet, but free for the first time in his life, he ran, and she followed. Achilles ran right into a pack of ravenous werewolves, with Yarra close behind.'

'I thought Jibrayne was a vampire,' Kelly said.

'She is,' Ray said. 'The werewolves were hunting her. Jibrayne at the time was probably the same age as we are now. Yarra had never seen a vampire before. We, the Rainbow, had never let her come in contact with any monster, so when she saw Jibrayne cowering from the werewolves, she thought she was just another girl. Yarra helped her, dragged her away from the werewolves. While Achilles held them off, the two fled.'

'They were friends?' Annika asked incredulously.

Again, Ray nodded. 'Our father found her about a week later. House Green was in chaos by then. All of the Rainbow was. We had lost the heir to House White. Her parents were calling for blood, but he found her a week later, still hiding with Jibrayne. The vampires were looking for them as well though. The vampires found them first, took both Yarra and Jibrayne deep into their coven. It was there Father found her and fought tooth and nail to get her out.'

'Jibrayne did nothing to help?' Matt asked with a slight frown of his own.

'She had no standing in the coven at that time,' Ray said. 'She was lucky to be allowed to live after what she did to Yarra.'

'But Jibrayne and Yarra remained close friends,' Kelly continued, 'until something happened.'

'So who are Lola and Lorelai?' Annika asked.

'As Jibrayne rose through her coven ranks, eventually gaining a coven of her own, she gained two trusted underlings,' Ray said distractedly. Something was wrong. 'Unfortunately, they are as devoted as they are deranged.'

He had stopped completely now, the jump incomplete, and stood turning in a circle staring into the sky. Something was very wrong.

'What is it?' Kelly asked.

The question answered itself a moment later as the green ring Ray wore flashed. The ring was one worn by any in service to the Rainbow; it signified their allegiance and the house to whom they served. Kelly, Matt and Annika each had their own rings; theirs were flashing too. That could only mean one thing: someone had called a meeting of all seven houses. A convergence was about to take place.

'So it begins,' Matt said.

Ray met the emerald eyes of his siblings with sadness but also strength, strength that was a promise, a promise they would get through this, that they would remain strong and together despite the fact that by the time they reached the convergence, Royce would have stolen leadership of House Green and none of them would have a home anymore.

A sickening sensation nestled deep in Ray's gut, a sickness that was both extremely painful and a blessing, a warning that the one they had pledged to protect was in pain – but alive. One single pained glance at his siblings confirmed it. The others had felt it too. Yarra needed them now.

Rule Seven. They were so close.

The Rainbow would have to wait.

29

Destroy

Pain was no stranger to one who had lived a life as full of questionable activities as she had. She knew it in all its shapes and forms. She knew all the masks and guised pain used to slip undetected into her life and the lives of those she cared for. Pain was an old friend, her oldest and dearest friend.

There was the pain she had grown up with, the pain of growing up entirely alone, of growing up behind closed doors, never having seen the sun or the stars or the sky. Then there was the pain of learning to talk only after her twentieth year because before there had been no need, the pain of taking ten years to learn the words and another five learning to hide them.

It was the pain of learning that others did not see what she did, that others did not know, as she knew, what was to come. They feared her knowledge of it, and so she was forced, through pain and suffering, to hide the knowledge that came so naturally to her, to use that to form the unshakable Rule One.

The next pain was masked with shock. In hindsight, Yarra was certain the reason she had run screaming through the Ivy Library until her parents grabbed her and forced her to calm down was because of the shock, not the actual pain. Screaming and with tears pouring down her face, Yarra had shown her parents the tiny puncture wound in her thumb and the single bead of bright red blood that dripped from it. Her demon hound Achilles, then a puppy, had bitten her. That had been the first time she had seen blood, any blood, and it had been her own.

But that didn't mean she liked it or relished its coming. She in no way enjoyed being coated in her own blood or having wounds so deep, pale bone could be seen through the red. It was not fun. It hurt. It hurt a lot. The only upside, if indeed there was one, was that the pain reminded her that she was still alive, reminded her that her existence meant something, that she was not trapped in a padded room with no one and nothing for comfort.

But Yarra White had learnt to deal with the pain. She was an assassin, a professional killer and procurer of hard-to-come-by information and artefacts. Anything they did to her, she could do to others. It was one way she coped, how she could bear the torture over and over, the locked rooms, and the centuries of silence. What she relished was the creative ways she could cause this same pain to others. It didn't matter how long it took. She was guaranteed years and years of time. Anything they did to her, she could do to others.

What made her smile, despite the punctured lung that made breathing more painful than life itself, was the joy she got from planning her revenge, every slow, sweet moment of it. It kept her going, those thoughts. Rule Five demanded revenge, but planning it was just as fun – that and the fact that it was genuinely quite amusing to watch the vampire sisters work together.

'Do the other one, do the other one, do the other one!' Lola cackled, her pink hair flying about her small head like confetti.

Lorelai grinned and bought Yarra's own dagger down on her. It sunk through her thigh like a hot knife through butter. Yarra screamed, spraying the sisters with blood, blood they licked daintily off their fingers, eyes closing as they tasted it, the power it contained, her screams music to their ears.

Lorelai didn't stop there. The vampire dragged the dagger down, cleaving open Yarra's muscle from the top of her thigh to her knee, the cut a mirror to the one on her other leg. Both gashes gaped like mouths; blood dribbled and bubbled over the lip of each, tracing warm tracks down her calves and splattering onto the floor, the splatters fast becoming a pool.

Tied to the chair as she was, wrists bound to the arms and her legs shackled to the legs of the chair, Yarra could do nothing as Lola grabbed her right leg. Her tongue forked out, lapping at the trails of blood, following them from her ankle up her leg. The pink-haired vampire bounced with excitement, her enthusiasm overflowing in giggles and high-pitched squeaks. Lola peered at the gash in Yarra's leg with barely disguised hunger. Then the vampire buried her head in the open wound.

Lorelai managed to restrain herself for a full second before she buried her head in the wound on Yarra's left leg. Like grotesque leeches, the sisters clung to her as she screamed.

Yarra arched back, hissing through her teeth at the mix of pain and pleasure she felt. Both vampire sisters rubbed themselves against her legs, coating themselves in her blood, lapping it up from where it gushed. Lola clamped her lips over the edge of the wound, fangs sinking into Yarra's bloody muscle. The vampire moaned, panting. Yarra arched again, straining against the ropes pulled tight with unnatural strength and the iron woven into it, straining even as the ropes tore her skin around the Rowan ash and iron bracelets she still wore.

'More . . .,' Lorelai moaned, pulling herself over Yarra's lap and clawing at her sister. 'More . . . more . . . more.'

Shoved off her food, Lola snarled. Blood dribbled from her mouth, down her chin.

'She's mine. I want her.'

'You had the other,' Lorelai slurred, fingers and fangs buried in bloodied flesh. 'This one's mine.'

'But you said I had to wait!' Lola whined. 'You said I had to wait until the others got here, to make them watch. It's not fair!'

Yarra flexed again, eyes darting to Erryk in the corner, and reached through the haze of pain towards the shadows. She clawed at them, drew as many to her as she could, scooping them towards her conscious mind, clawing at the sea of power until she had enough to use – barely.

Arms suddenly free, she lurched forward, smacking Lorelai's blood-splattered blue head with her own. Stunned, the vampire rolled from her lap, slapping her pink-haired sister squarely in the jaw with her fist.

Lola blinked once. Lorelai stared, unblinking. The vampire sisters snarled in unison. Yarra, panting and drenched head to foot in her own blood, snarled back.

Then they were pouncing at each other, the vampire sisters launching forward, fangs and claw like hands prepared to rip, shred, and tear. Yarra simply toppled. Her arms free, she launched herself forward, but her ankles were still bound to the chair, and any strength she channelled to her legs flowed from her wounds in torrents. So she toppled, tripping over her tied feet and clattering face first into the floor. She lay there, face down, groaning.

Lola and Lorelai stopped their advance. They stood shoulder to shoulder and stared down at her, something like confusion written on their blood-coated faces.

'*What was that?*' Lola asked through bubbling, gurgling laughs. The laughs did nothing to cover the genuine curiosity in her red eyes or the way she held her head cocked to the side, as if she truly did not know what to make of this latest development.

'I think, sister mine,' Lorelai drawled, prowling closer to her downed prey, looking equally as confused as her sister, 'that that was supposed to be an escape attempt.'

'But it failed.' Lola looked genuinely concerned. 'I thought Jibrayne said she was smart. Wasn't she smarter than this last time?'

Crashes and screams from beyond. The sounds of fighting drawing ever closer. The sisters didn't seem to hear.

'She was smarter than this, you're right,' Lorelai said with a frown. 'Maybe it's the blood loss. Remember the other one? He fell too once we emptied him. And he was so strong.'

Yarra tried to push herself up, to right the chair with her still in it. She got as far as raising her head before it all became too much, and she pressed her cheek to the floor again.

'Poor baby can't move,' Lorelai cooed. 'What should we do to this poor baby?'

She snarled at them with as much feral animosity as her pain-hazed mind could muster.

'Can I eat her?' Lola asked. 'Can I? can I? Please, please, please?'

'But she's all dirty,' Lorelai said reasonably. 'You'll get sick.'

Lola shrugged. 'We can clean her, tie her up like the other one, and dunk her in the river.'

'We can't do that, Lola. The river will wash all the blood away.'

Lola hung her head. 'Oh.'

Yarra forced a small cough, brought blood bubbling through her lips with the effort. The sisters swung impatient faces her way. Red eyes narrowed.

'Hold her up,' Lorelai snapped.

Pouting, Lola did as she was bid. The tiny pink-haired vampire hooked her spindle-thin arms under Yarra's shoulders and heaved her upright. Hands clasped behind Yarra's head, the vampire held her tight while her sister prowled closer still.

'I'm going to drain you dry, girl,' she hissed.

Yarra snorted, heaved, 'Jibrayne won't like that.'

'To hell with Jibrayne. Actually, to hell with everything. I'm hungry.'

Lorelai smiled sweetly, the motion lost in the coating of blood plastered over her face. The vampire licked her lips, her tongue running over her fangs, pausing over the tip of each as she eyed the exposed portion of Yarra's neck. Hesitation lasted less than a heartbeat before those fangs were buried to the gums in pulsing lifeblood.

Yarra wanted to scream, to snarl, to sob, to do anything other than hang there like she was now. Vampire venom worked in a strange way. Their bite was as painful as one would expect. Having fangs sunk into tender flesh was understandably and expectedly painful, but that wasn't the problem. The problem was the paralysing effect their bite had, a toxin that, once injected into the bloodstream of their victim, kept them motionless and in a strange state of bliss – strange because the euphoria the toxin caused could not cancel out the pain of the initial bite or any number of bites to follow.

She may have wanted to scream and curse and fight, but the amount of blood she'd already lost was approaching the very worst she had ever experienced, and that, coupled with this new dose of vampire toxin, left Yarra almost unable to do anything.

She could always heal herself, rid herself of the toxin, replenish the blood she had lost, and close those gaping wounds in her thighs, but healing took so much more effort and concentration than anyone realised or gave her credit for. Plus, she was chained in iron again. She still wore her Rowan ash and iron bracelets. Her magic was stifled.

Besides, she hated healing herself, couldn't rationalise the need to. All her life, she had been protected and coddled and told her life was worth more than those of her friends and the family she had chosen to value. Every single injury had always been healed for her. Even the smallest of paper cuts were sealed with the quick remorseless magic of those sworn to protect her. There had never been nor would there ever be any reason to heal her own wounds when she didn't also have to heal someone else.

Besides, they were almost here. The sounds of fighting had almost stopped, the clash of weapons on weapons so close, she could almost taste it. All she had to do was keep the sisters' attention focussed on her for just a moment longer . . .

She had done the hard part. She had found Erryk and kept Lola and Lorelai occupied long enough for the others to arrive. She had done her part. All that remained was to wait for them to arrive.

And there it was – the bang, clash of the door being broken down and the rescue forces filing in. Yarra made her move, a move driven by pure desperation, clutching at straws and remnants of the power hidden from her by the toxin.

She scissored her legs, breaking them free from the chains, kicking Lorelai's out from under her. She bucked forward, lurching Lola with her, and sank her own teeth into the vampire. She ripped out a chink of Lorelai's neck and spat it at her sister before biting a finger off the hands that still held her. Then she was free and twisting, a hand reaching up to her midnight hair and ripping free Myrthos in one smooth movement.

'Took you long enough,' she rasped, swaying where she stood, head so clouded, she wasn't sure it was actually him until he spoke.

'Sorry, but we did have to fight our way in,' Ray spat back.

Yarra smiled at him and at the siblings who fanned out around him, weapons dripping blood and emerald eyes glinting like shards of ice. Her own stone-cold eyes flicked towards Erryk, unconscious in a heap where the sisters had left him discarded like a rag.

'Did you kill them all?' she asked sweetly.

'Every single stinking one of them,' Annika answered, running over to Erryk, sheathing her blood-splattered twin rapiers as she went.

Kelly and Matt levelled weapons at the last remaining vampires in the castle complex. Ray joined them, eyes on Annika and Erryk.

'Did they bite him?' he asked.

Annika shook her head, pure mahogany hair swishing with the movement. Relief coloured her voice. 'No.'

'I told you, you should have let me eat him when we had the chance,' Lola whined, seemingly unaware of the malice directed her way. 'I told you, I told you, and you didn't listen to me.'

Ray turned his piercing eyes on Yarra, scanning the blood, the shake of her muscles as she tried to bully them into keeping her standing, the blood.

'Did they bite you?' he asked.

She didn't answer, only snapped Myrthos out of its whip form into the razor-sharp rapier and levelled it at the vampires.

One flick from the tip had Kelly and Matt stepping back, the twins with Ray making a barrier between them and Erryk. A second twitch had Lola and Lorelai scrambling for fallen swords, real fear in their eyes as they recognised that, at last, she had gone over the edge.

'If you live,' Yarra trilled, her head tilted to the side, exposing the wound on her neck and the blood that bubbled free, 'tell Jibrayne I say hi.'

30

Treason

The peacekeepers ruled the government. House Blue practically controlled the whole of Verstra's politics. They were neutral, the link between the Rainbow and the rest of Verstran society. The convergence always convened there. There was safety in the anonymity of government meetings and policy-making procedures. While Verstra was ruled from the chambers above, the Rainbow met in secret below, ensuring the safety of this world from the shadows, making sure that the laws made above ground still had people to protect in the future.

The council room was a large underground dome, ceilings several times higher than they ought to have been spanned by arching bridges of stone intricately carved with swirls and memorabilia reflecting the houses beneath. Seven colossal doorways bordered the underground room, one door for each house. Behind each, the leaders of the most powerful houses in Verstra assembled with their advisors and armies.

Soon, they would walk through their respective doors and take their places in the convergence. Each lord or leader would stand at the head of their house and move to take a seat at the table. The table had one seat per house, a ring of carved wood within the larger ring of the convergence.

Royce had never given much thought to the single swivel chair placed dead centre in the room, surrounded on all sides by the extremely powerful members of the Rainbow. But now it occurred to him that seat was reserved for the White. Seat them in the centre of the convergence, surrounded on all sides by those who had pledged to keep them from harm. Keep them caged, locked inside the wall of the Rainbow – safe.

Royce was the last to arrive, but that had been intentional. He had held the armies of House Green behind their door until he was sure all the other houses had arrived. He wanted to see how the others would react to a council called by a lowly captain of the guard.

Ferric Oxblood wore his red cloak with the hood down, allowing Royce to see the whole of his face and the deep scowl he wore across it. It also offered him a clear view of his blond hair, hair which lifted and crackled with unseen power, and piercing blue eyes that almost seemed to burn. Half a step behind him was his wife, Shaniqua, and the captain of his guard. Behind them was their army.

Alexander Sheresta loomed like a mountain at the head of House Orange. Hazel eyes met with Royce's for a brief second and warmed in satisfaction, his legendary grasp of tactics and battlefield manoeuvring clearly affording him a clear picture of what was about to occur. Half a step behind him stood his wife and captain. Royce's eyes caught on the small girl held close to Theresa Sheresta in a vice-like grip.

Had her silver-white hair not given her away then, the flame-fed eyes that burned like tiny pinprick fires did. They had brought along Izrabella Dijon, the shivering girl wrapped in an orange scarf, the only piece of her family's heritage she was allowed to keep.

House Yellow had no army behind them, but Royce knew the people crowded behind Charlotte Goldenrod were more powerful than any army. Two pairs of golden eyes burned from behind Charlotte, her tall bald captain of the guard loomed off to one side, Charlotte's partner, Charles, with him. The scores of branch family members they had brought in lieu of an army scowled at Royce and the green cape he wore, twin to the yellow one Charlotte was cloaked in.

Dean and Lynda Couvrette smiled warmly at Royce. Their sword master grinned openly, proudly displaying the sword she wore at her waist, knowing full well that none could challenge her and live to tell the tale. Off to the side, flanked by armed guards, stood Meredith and Taiga Beryl; their blue cloaks confiscated after their loss of power, they each wore sashes of blue at their waists.

Joseph and Julie Moon of House Indigo stood proud and alert. They too smiled at Royce, grins that spoke volumes of their pride and triumph at the victory to come. The armies of House Indigo fanned out behind them, two figures corralled in the centre, surrounded on all sides by soldiers with their hands suspiciously close to their weapons. Royce stared, blinked once, and stared some more.

Twin pairs of mismatched eyes glinted, one crystal blue, the other forest green. Davinder Aster, with his green-streaked dusty blond hair, coated in dirt, grime, and soot, fiddled with a metallic cube in his hands. Katya Aster, with her purple-streaked hair, looked no different. Both wore sashes of indigo pink. Davinder wore his around his neck like an ascot; Katya wore hers atop her head. Both were stained and smeared with soot. Both twitched with nervous energy. Both shouldn't have been there.

Royce frowned. It was highly unusual for the surviving members of displaced families to be at convergence meetings, stranger still that Izrabella and the Aster siblings were here and not secreted away in whatever hideout they lived in, locked away from the rest of the world until they were all but forgotten, strange that all the leaders of the other houses seemed to know what was going to happen before he told them, like they had been expecting it and dragged along the disposed of originals to humiliate them further.

He didn't mind though. It was good to have a more appreciative audience. What he had to say about the pledge would be better understood by them.

Kayneth Kor grinned, the scar that ran the length of his left side contorting it into a sneer of grotesque monstrosity, his hard eyes alight with excitement, cherry-gold hair gleaming. His family flanked him, the dark rust colour of his children's hair gleaming like dried blood. The tall hawk-like woman who commanded their armies peered down at them, all through the pair of glasses perched on her long hooked nose. No Amaryllis family members lived to bear the purple sash of their house.

The lords and leaders of the other houses glanced once at one another before, as one, taking a step forward and sitting in their appointed seats.

'Thank you all for coming on such short notice,' Royce said loudly, stepping forward, Ray's cloak swishing behind him as he took Ray's appointed seat.

'*What is the meaning of this?*' Ferric Oxblood demanded, flames crackling around him and his army, flaring up from clenched fists as he slammed them down on the table.

'Where is Lord Mossman and his family?' Charlotte Goldenrod interjected, voice hard, a phantom wind extinguishing Ferric's hands.

'Ray Mossman has run off on a ludicrous vendetta against the vampires. He declared war on them!' Royce shouted above the rising din.

'Why would he do that?' Ferric asked.

'And the girl?' Charlotte asked, a frantic note turning her usually calm voice up in pitch, the air in the room suddenly thin. 'What of the girl?'

Royce ignored them both. 'Ray Mossman has shown himself to be possessed of poor judgement. Declaring war on the vampires when they had none nothing to prompt such extreme action.'

'They are monsters!' Alexander Sheresta called loudly. 'As lord of House Green, he is, technically, within his rights to declare war on them.'

'It is foolishness!' Ferric shouted. 'He should know to never, never even think about war. Especially not with the girl in his care.'

'Why not?' Dean Couvrette asked in what appeared to be a perfectly reasonable tone. 'Isn't that why we pulled her from Trepidation?'

'We agreed she would advise,' Ferric said, voice tight, face pale. 'Fighting was never part of the plan.'

'You would deprive the Rainbow of her skills as a fighter,' Alexander Sheresta asked, 'purposefully weaken the Rainbow in this way?'

Ferric said nothing, face still pale. Charlotte Goldenrod too was pale beneath her halo of dark unruly curls.

Royce's eyes sparkled. 'Speaking of the girl,' he said sweetly, 'I have uncovered some very interesting information regarding her and her connection to the Rainbow.' He waited until silence had fallen and all eyes were on him before adding, 'And the simple fact alone that Ray would declare war on one small vampire faction when there is a much larger war looming should be grounds enough for his removal as lord of House Green.'

'You have no right!' Charlotte screamed at him. 'You have no right to ask such a thing! Or to call a convergence in the first place!'

'There's more,' Royce said firmly. 'I have proof that the Mossman family, also families Oxblood and Goldenrod – in fact, all the so-called original families – have been jeopardising the safety and integrity of the Rainbow for generations.'

Ferric and Charlotte froze. In the silence that followed, Kayneth's grin looked like one of a wolf. The leaders of the other houses seemed to lean forward, eager to hear this latest of revelations.

'First,' Royce began, smiling, 'the girl you all risked your lives to free from Trepidation is, in fact, Yarra White.'

'This is not groundbreaking news, boy,' Ferric snapped. 'We would not have freed her otherwise.'

Royce nodded. 'Agreed, but do any of you know the circumstances that led to her incarceration in the halls in the first place?'

Silence in the room.

'I thought not,' Royce said, 'because it is a mystery. All I could find in all the history books and court rulings housed in House Green, the keeper of knowledge, was that she murdered her parents. Murdered her parents and then slaughtered a good number of House Blue's personal guards to make her escape. And do you know what punishment she received once the Rainbow caught her?'

The leaders of the other houses were looking at him strangely.

He gave them a small grin. 'She was banished,' he said with a flourish. 'Banished. Not executed, as the punishment for murdering members of the Rainbow demands, but banished.'

'She had connections,' Kayneth Kor said, brow creased. 'I remember the ruling. She had connections even then.'

Royce looked to Dean Couvrette. That ruling and the events that immediately followed had seen him appointed leader of House Blue, had seen Meredith and Taiga Beryl removed from power.

'Why banish someone you know has no qualms killing members of the Rainbow?' Royce asked. 'Why banish such a dangerous individual instead of killing her outright?'

'She had connections . . .,' Kayneth said again, although he didn't sound sure.

'What if I told you that the very existence of the Rainbow, the very foundation of the organisation we all have devoted our lives to, rests on the life of one individual?' Royce asked. 'Would her strange sentencing make sense then?'

Utter silence greeted his words.

'That all members of these original families have pledged to protect this one individual with their lives, to value the life of this one person over their own, sacrificing anything and everything to keep this one individual alive – would it make sense then?'

'And who is this person?' Kayneth asked, hard eyes narrowed but understanding and dread beginning to show in his face.

Royce smirked. 'I have learned that should this individual die, the collective power of the Rainbow would fade, wane, and eventually vanish altogether. Because of the pledge the original families made to this one individual, if they were to die, the lives of every single family member from every single family would be forfeit as well. The Rainbow would fall in an instant.'

'Preposterous!' Alexander Sheresta spat. 'There is no way anyone of an original family or not would take such a large risk. No way that such a pledge would be allowed to be made. Such a cost is not worth it, no matter the presumed importance of the individual.'

Royce knew he had won the moment he said, 'If you don't believe me, ask them.'

Ferric Oxblood and Charlotte Goldenrod had gone pale. All the blood had drained from their faces, and they swayed in their seats. Izrabella Dijon was trying to hide behind Theresa Sheresta. The Beryls looked like they were trying to disappear. The Aster siblings were still, all nervous energy stolen from them in an instant. That alone was proof enough. He had won.

'But if the Rainbow's power really would fade with this individual's death,' Dean Couvrette mused, 'then such a risk would be worth it.'

'If such an individual were to exist,' Alexander Sheresta said, 'they should be contained in a secure location. Provided protection around the clock and never let out of our sight. Such a person would be known throughout the Rainbow, their protection given the highest priority.'

'That we know nothing of this seems to speak against its validity,' Joseph Moon finished.

Royce nodded. 'But what better protection is there than secrecy? What better place to hide someone than behind myth and mystery? What better protection is there than to let them lose in a world that knows nothing about them?'

Alexander Sheresta held up a hand. 'Are you saying that the person the original families of the Rainbow have pledged their lives to protect . . . is Yarra White?'

'Criminal, thief, and murderer Yarra White,' Royce confirmed. 'She killed her own parents, a crime that would usually be punished with immediate execution, but because of the pledge the esteemed lords swore to her, she was let off. Banished but not killed. They let a known killer, a ruthless, heartless killer, walk free! What's more, they released her from their protection, allowed her to run amok with monsters and rebel militias, knowing full well that her death would destroy the Rainbow. *They must be stopped!*'

Royce could only smile at the roar of approval this brought.

'The many wrongdoings Ray has committed and the fact that his own loyal guard – the soldiers that have served House Green for centuries – are here with me rather than fighting his ridiculous vendetta against the vampires prove he is unfit to rule. I move for the immediate removal of Ray Mossman as lord of House Green!' Royce called.

Four voices rose in agreement. Two stayed silent.

'In light of new revelations concerning this so-called pledge, perhaps it would be wise to remove Ferric Oxblood and Charlotte Goldenrod from power as well,' Kayneth Kor mused loudly. 'This way, even if the girl were to meet her end, the Rainbow would have a strong foundation within which to rebuild.'

'Especially with war coming,' Joseph Moon added. 'It seems foolish to leave half our strength dependent on the life of one girl. Especially if we expect her to fight for us.'

Royce nodded earnestly. 'I would not have bought it to your attention if I thought otherwise.'

'All those in favour of removing Ray Mossman from power effective immediately?' Alexander Sheresta asked.

Royce raised his hand, as did Joseph Moon, Kayneth Kor, and Dean Couvrette.

Alexander Sheresta nodded, raised his own hand, and said, 'Motion carried.'

Royce swelled with pride. He had won. He was in charge now. He had uprooted the Mossmans. He had won.

'As to the removal of Ferric Oxblood and Charlotte Goldenrod' – Alexander raised a hand for silence – 'they shall remain in power until suitable replacements can be found. Whether that be before or after this war is won remains to be seen. All in favour?'

Again, another overwhelming vote of agreement.

'Congratulations, Royce. You are now leader of House Green.'

31

Games

Yarra could barely stand. He could see it in the shake and wobble of her legs, those ghastly gashes gurgling up the last vestiges of her blood. Her thighs quivered like wet noodles, utterly unable to support her weight, yet she forced herself to remain standing. Every breath brought a wince past her lips. She was hunched slightly over to the side, bent into the pain.

It hurt him, physically, to see her like this. It was his duty to protect her, his duty to keep her from harm. He had failed to uphold the pledge in all its grotesque and outdated glory; simply for allowing Yarra to be injured should have resulted in his death. But the pledge had been altered since Yarra. It was an unwritten agreement among all the surviving members of the original families; as long as Yarra survived, she was allowed to do as she wished.

And if she wished to get herself killed by these lunatic vampire sisters, then so be it. He would let her fight them, let her work through her anger. Erryk was alive and unharmed, the other vampires dead. If Yarra wished to fight Lola and Lorelai despite her obvious weakness just to taunt Jibrayne and the monster armies her old friend had poised to destroy them all, then so be it.

Ray would let her have her fun and only step in if she really was about to die.

There was a smile on her face. Despite the blood all over her and smeared through her hair, the bright white flash of teeth was clear, and she gripped Myrthos firmly. Ray knew there was nothing he could do to stop her. He only prayed she'd still be alive by the end of it or that he had the ability to step in and force them apart before this went too far.

Lola sprang towards Yarra, fangs dripping with blood and spittle, blood-coated blades flashing forward. Her bright pink hair was streaked with deep red; from roots to tips, pink and red merged, swam together as the small vampire flew through the air with preternatural speed. Similarly but also in stark contrast was her sister. Lorelai's blue hair was coated in the stuff, the half-smile she wore on her face directed more towards her sister than the girl before them.

Ray watched them fight with fascinated horror. He had seen Yarra fight before – one could not be her friend without doing so – but not for years. And it had been almost a lifetime since he had seen her fight for the pure pleasure of it.

He hated that she liked it, hated himself for allowing her only pleasure to come from putting herself in life or death situations, hated that it was, at least in part, his fault she was like this. It was his deepest shame, that he had not helped her back then, that he had allowed her to become this way, that he hadn't been able to show her that life was worth living.

Lorelai and Lola pounced on her, lunged with vampire swiftness, stabbing with daggers, knives, and swords, discarding each weapon moments after they were acquired.

The sisters coordinated their movements expertly. It was a wonder to watch. As Lola dived for Yarra's weakened legs, Lorelai went high or from behind, waiting in Yarra's blind spot to attack. Such masterful teamwork was simply stunning to witness. It required one to have complete trust in the other. Teamwork such as that left no room for doubt. They were spectacular and unstoppable.

Yarra was better, dodging each and every sword thrust, knife swing, and perfectly timed combo move. Despite the injuries she had sustained, she swung Myrthos with expert precision, its thin rapier blade deflecting every blade she did not dodge and skewering the vampire sisters whenever they got too close. Then suddenly, the vampires backed off.

Chests heaving and eyes narrowed, they surveyed there would be prey.

'Can't we eat them?' Lola asked.

Lorelai gave a short nod. 'House Green does taste the best.'

Ray didn't even have time to flinch, to grip his sword any tighter in preparation for a fight before crack. In an instant, Yarra had flicked Myrthos out of its rapier form back into the whip and cracked it at the vampire sisters.

'I'm not done playing yet,' she drawled in an eerie mockery of Lola's own whine.

Now Yarra was on the offensive, springing towards Lorelai like a cat. The vampire dodged and retaliated with inhuman strength and speed, but Yarra let her momentum carry her, let herself hang airborne and defenceless for a moment before touching lightly down on the ground and instantly folding into a roll. It was a move so perfect, so flawlessly infallible that one could be forgiven for thinking she had not thrown herself into a roll at all but collapsed in utter exhaustion as her body screamed against the exertion she forced upon it.

She bought Myrthos around in a sweep, scissoring her legs in the opposite direction. A hand connected with Lorelai's head, fingers twisted in blue hair, and suddenly, Yarra had the upper hand, Lorelai's head yanked back in a death grip, Myrthos levelled at Lola's chest.

'Try harder,' Yarra wheezed and threw Lorelai at her sister's feet.

The vampires growled, the feral sound the only warning they gave.

Yarra spun, twirling in a complete circle, balanced on one leg, slicing Myrthos behind her. She spun and then launched herself into a dive. A yell fought past her lips as Lola's broken talon-like nails clipped her heel.

As suddenly as it had started, it was over. Lorelai had her hand fisted in Yarra's night-black hair, her head yanked back, and Lola hovered close by, fangs poised to sink into flesh.

'*Yarra!*' Annika shrieked, abandoning Erryk as she hurried forward.

'Uh-uh-uh-ah,' Lorelai tutted, yanking Yarra's head farther back. 'One more step, and Little Missy here gets it.'

Lola was all but panting over Yarra's neck, over the place where her pulse throbbed with the last of its strength as her chest heaved in great lungfuls of air and eyes shot cold hard daggers their way.

'Jibrayne . . . would . . . be so . . . proud,' Yarra gasped out.

'Oh, you bet.' Lorelai giggled. 'We're her top lieutenants now.'

Yarra raised an eyebrow, straining slightly to gaze at the vampire. 'Really? I thought you already were.'

Lorelai nodded, but her eyes flashed. 'Saw that,' she said.

And before Ray could so much as draw breath, to clench his fingers around his sword, to ready himself to charge forward, Lola had sunk her fangs into Yarra's neck.

Annika and Kelly screamed. Matt cursed loudly. Yarra closed her eyes and groaned.

Ray had enough time to sink into utter despair, to look to his family with nothing but sorrow in his eyes, a sorrow so profound that although none of them met his eyes, they all felt it through their core, a sense that this was the end, that they would all die here in this dark, dank castle of a stronghold, to become the food for the vampires as they prepared to destroy everything they had spent their lives protecting.

He had enough time to wish things had been different, to wish he had acted differently, to wish he had been there with her when she had needed him most, to wish he had been there the night she slaughtered her parents, to stop her or help her, he didn't know. Ray only knew he wished he had been there. He had been too late to save her then, to save her from herself and the monsters she had deluded herself into seeing, had been too late to save her when the lords banished her, had been too late to save her now.

If only he had jumped in, stopped the fight before it had begun. Eyes moist, he couldn't help but think this could all have been avoided, all this heartache and pain avoided if only he had done one simple thing. Yarra herself had known, had asked, 'Have I been bound?' and he had told her no. Perhaps if he had bound her to the library walls, bound her to his presence, she would not have gone out on her own, would not have challenged a castle full of vampires, and would not be lying dead at their feet.

Only she wasn't.

Ray looked, blinked, and then looked again, and she simply wasn't there. He really should have known better.

The vampire sisters were frozen in place. One joint popped and then another and another until Lola blinked, Lorelai blinked, and both scowled at the space Yarra had occupied moments before.

'Where –'

Lola opened her mouth, only to have the tip of Myrthos protrude from her lips. She spat blood onto her sister's face.

Lorelai had a hand pressed to her throat, lips opening and closing like a fish before she crumpled, simply dropped to the ground, unblinking eyes staring up. Lola landed in a heap beside her, fingers stretching for her sister. Lorelai's limp hand fell away from her neck, and Ray gaped at the hole left behind.

Yarra withdrew Myrthos with a sick wet slurping bubble and grinned, night black falling away from her face like water to reveal pearl-white teeth stained red and clamped tight around a quivering chunk of flesh. Smirking, she spat it out and stalked closer, kneeling before the vampire sisters with an ease that, given her injuries, should not have been possible.

'Jibrayne's set it into motion, hasn't she?' she asked. 'She's prepared?'

Lorelai dipped her chin slightly, ever so slightly so as not to encourage more of her blood to leave her body.

'After all this time. Why now?'

'Trepidation was not just for us, was it?' Ray asked, moving to catch her as Yarra swayed and then collapsed completely.

Yarra shook her head. 'They and you could not get to me. It might have been the one place I was truly safe.'

Ray very much doubted that. 'Heal yourself, Yarra,' he said. 'Heal yourself, or it will be worse for you.'

'I know,' she said eyes, closing. 'I refuse.'

Ray sighed; he had guessed as much. 'Annika, make sure these two don't leave any time soon!' he barked. 'Kelly, Matt, carry Erryk. We're leaving.'

Ray assessed Yarra's numerous wounds. The more serious ones, he bound in hastily grown lichen moss, stifling the bleeding. He scooped Yarra up like a child and then, at Annika's unasked question, added, 'Don't kill them. If they really are Jibrayne's lieutenants like they claim, it will be useful to have them owe us.'

Annika nodded, face ghastly pale. Kelly and Matt too had all colour drained from their faces. Ray supposed he didn't look much different. No more blood seeped from Yarra's wounds, the floors coated with all her small body had to give.

There was only one place he could take her now, one place he could take her if they stood any chance of surviving this along with her, one person who could do the impossible and bring her back from the brink. It didn't matter that that person happened to presently be in the company of that traitor or that to appear before the both of them now, with Yarra as she was, would most likely mean their death in any case. He had no choice.

His siblings formed a circle around him, Annika to his right, emerald eyes fixed on the slow rise and fall of Yarra's chest, Kelly and Matt, with Erryk limp between them, to his left. They stood as close as they dared, elbows and shoulders touching, sharing their collective power for the jump.

'Hurry,' Ray said. 'We must get to the convergence at once.'

32

Consequences

'Next order of business should be to assign more guards to House Green, to . . . aid with the transition.' Alexander Sheresta smiled warmly towards Royce.

The newly minted leader of House Green grinned back.

'Ray-Ray should be told,' Charlotte Goldenrod called, voice shaking but strong even as her face paled further, and she leaned heavily on the back of her seat. 'The Mossmans have a right to know that they no longer have a home.'

'What is to stop them residing at the Ivy Library?' Ferric Oxblood asked. 'Every house needs the presence of a founding family.'

Kayneth Kor and Alexander Sheresta exchanged a look. Royce tried to read what passed between them, the meaning behind that look.

'The Mossmans are too numerous to be allowed to reside in the library,' Kayneth said. 'Ray will no doubt appeal this ruling, and should he choose to do so, it would be better for all involved if he was not so close to his old seat of power.'

'You think Ray would . . . attack his own soldiers?' Charlotte called, aghast, her voice strange and choked as she hissed through her teeth and clutched at her chest, 'Attack his own home and endanger the lives of his siblings?'

She broke off with a gasp, hand pressed firmly to her chest, over her heart. Terrified golden eyes locked on Ferric, her mouth forming words Royce couldn't hear. Ferric Oxblood was shaking, shoulders hunched inward as he clawed at the front of his red cloak.

Startled, Royce rose from his seat, questions burning on his lips as the armies of Houses Red and Yellow surged forward towards their lords. What was going on?

His ears caught a startled sob from House Orange. His eyes sought out the girl straining against the claw-like grip of Theresa Sheresta, tears streaming down her face as she grabbed at herself and pulled against the hands that held her. A low moan from House Indigo. The two remaining Asters doubled over behind the wall of Joseph Moon's guards, Davinder and Katya Aster leaning on each other as they groaned and moaned in agony.

Royce cast his eyes to the Beryls, where they too were pressing white-knuckled hands to their chests, breaths coming in shallow gasps, eyes darting all over the room, fixing on the other members of the original families.

What had happened?

'It's Yarra,' Zenon whispered hoarsely. 'She's in trouble.'

Royce didn't question how Zenon knew, not when he too rubbed the spot over his heart and his face contorted in pain.

'You took the pledge?' he hissed through clenched teeth.

The old soldier nodded. 'All those who know the truth take the pledge. She's in trouble.'

Zenon crept back to the ranks of the soldiers, and Royce once again turned his attention to the convergence.

'We will deal with the Mossmans,' Alexander said as if nothing had happened and he hadn't noticed both Charlotte and Ferric doubling over in pain. 'Once it becomes apparent whether they survived their ill-fated attack on the vampires, we will deal with them.'

Ferric and Charlotte lurched forward at once. Both leapt from their appointed seats and vaulted over the circular table, both rushing for the centre of the room where the air seemed to ripple and warp.

Amidst the shouts and sudden uproar from the other leaders, Royce saw the air tear and split, saw five figures tumble through the space between and land heavily on the ground.

Five figures: Kelly and Matt, with a limp Erryk between them, Annika, and Ray.

No sign of the girl.

Annika's frilly war dress was torn, her twin rapiers dipped in blood like red ink, pigtails askew. Kelly and Matt carried Erryk between them, the twins' glares nothing short of menacing, but there was an undercurrent of fear, fear not only for the loss of their home, of their status and power, but also a deeper fear, fear of something much worse.

Royce looked at Ray again, really looked at him: the pale face, drawn lips, and sweat-beaded brow, the arms that trembled as they clutched the rags, the rags that shifted and moved, a night-black curtain that shifted to reveal a sliver of pale skin, half-cracked eyes of red rimmed grey, and a mouth hanging half open dyed brightest red.

Royce was aware too of the change in the room, for although the leaders of the houses were rising up in anger, the original leading families, the Goldenrods and Oxbloods and Asters and Beryls, had gone still.

Not a bundle of rags at all but a person – a person dying or already dead.

Charlotte and Ferric, both of who had surged forward as Ray jumped directly onto the council room, were still before him. Ferric's blue eyes and Charlotte's golden ones were fixed on Yarra.

Only one person moved forward, one person who was free of either the frozen shock or shocked outrage that gripped everyone else, one person who crept forward, whose silvery-white hair seemed to glow and who held out tiny shaking hands, one person who had lines of blood across her arms where Theresa's nails had torn through cloth and flesh.

'What happened?' Ferric Oxblood asked, his voice surprisingly soft and devoid of its usual fire.

'What do you think happened?' Ray shot back. Hard eyes passed right over Royce, failing to react in any way to the cape Royce wore, a twin to Ray's own.

'Does she still live?' Meredith Beryl asked.

Yarra rolled from Ray's arms, landing in a crouch on the floor. Blood sprayed and smeared behind her, leaving a thick trail in her wake.

'What do you take me for?' she asked, her voice scarcely above a whisper. 'Of course, I'm still alive.'

Yet even as she said this, she tried to rise; her legs shook and buckled and folded neatly under her. She fell forward, night-black hair once again covering her face.

'What is this anyway?' she asked. 'Was Royce successful?'

Izrabella Dijon, last surviving member of House Orange, climbed over the circular table. She scrambled past Alexander Sheresta without reacting to him in any way. She reached Yarra's form and placed a hand on her shoulder, enveloping her in the same silver light that surrounded her.

Before their very eyes, the one girl who could spell the end for all the Rainbow, the one girl whose very existence threatened to tear apart their entire organisation, began to heal.

What they needed was a fresh start. A fresh start for the entire Rainbow could only happen once all the members of the original families were dead. The Rainbow needed a fresh start. It needed to be strengthened from the ground up, rebuilt, stronger and better. That was the only way they'd win this war. The fastest way to achieve that was through the death of the girl, the girl who was healing before them, whose wounds were slowly closing up before their eyes. If only she were to die.

Clearly, what he had said had sunk in, the repercussions of the pledge not lost on the other house leaders. Royce saw every thought as it crossed their faces, saw it the moment each of them made their decisions.

Alexander Sheresta gripped knives in his hands. Theresa had curved daggers in hers. Lynda and Dean Couvrette, Joseph and Julie Moon and their daughter, Kayneth Kor, his wife, and children too all gripped weapons and were advancing on the pair of crouched girls. The Mossmans would pose no threat. It was clear they were all injured and exhausted. Should they all attack now, Yarra could be killed; the pledge would ensure a fresh start for the Rainbow.

Royce did not move to join them. He could not let them end her. He moved swift and true, darting before Kayneth with the unnatural quickness his magic afforded him.

'I know what you're thinking,' he said, 'but I cannot let you kill her.'

'You were the one who bought this grave misconduct to our attention, Royce,' Alexander Sheresta said. 'Why would you stop us?'

'If such an individual were to exist,' Joseph Moon said, 'if such an individual were to exist . . . You said that, Alexander. Those were your words. The existence of one such individual is now irrefutable. She lies before us now. And you would have us kill her?'

Joseph asked a genuine question. For although he had followed Kayneth Kor and Alexander Sheresta as they both grabbed weapons and advanced, it was clear he had listened more closely to what Royce had said about the pledge.

'It would only be them who would die,' Kayneth said, indicating the space in the centre of the room, the usually vacant space inside the circle of the polished wooden table presently occupied by almost all the surviving members of the original families. 'The Rainbow would remain strong,' Kayneth continued. 'We would remain strong, stronger even, now that the liability known as Yarra would be removed.'

A collective intake of breath from behind him. The air seemed to fizz and hiss. Heat pressed against the back of his neck, the very ground shook and heaved, but Royce stood firm. He had caused this. He would not let them kill her.

'We would all suffer,' he said firmly, noting with a touch of pride that Zenon and a few other high-ranking and trusted guards were stepping in to intercept the other leaders.

The shadows around the edge of the room seemed to rumble and laugh.

'*Were you not listening to a word he said?*' Ferric demanded, steam rising from his shoulders. 'Did you not listen to a word he said about the pledge? About why we've all dedicated our lives to keeping her safe?'

It was Ferric, more than anything Royce could have said, that perhaps gave them pause. Whether because of his overall presence or his crackling, sizzling magic, Royce didn't know, but Alexander, Kayneth, and Joseph stopped dead in their tracks.

'Well?' Ferric demanded. 'What did he say?'

Next to Ferric's blue-eyed fire, Charlotte looked as collected as ever, but her golden eyes burned. 'I may have been opposed to his appointment as leader, but the boy spoke masterfully about the pledge. He gave you all the facts, and yet you're all still stupid to see. If this is what the Rainbow has come to, perhaps we deserve to die.'

Royce could have kissed her – or slapped her. He wasn't sure the aid she provided outweighed the insult.

Kayneth scowled, his scar making his face nothing short of terrifying. '*I will not be treated like a child!*' he roared.

'Then answer the question,' Charlotte shot back, deadly calm, even though a phantom wind billowed around her, lifting her hair and sending whorls of Ferric's smoke tumbling through the room, seeping into those strange shadows and vanishing forever.

'If the individual were to die, the founders' magic would fade,' Alexander Sheresta said tightly, his hazel eyes burning from behind his mountain-like frame. 'The founders' magic. Not ours.'

'You stupid little worms,' Ferric spat, 'could you be any more dense?'

Royce turned to look at the lord of House Red. He and Charlotte stood shoulder to shoulder, facing Kayneth and Alexander. Meredith and Taiga Beryl faced Joseph Moon and the other armed combatants. Davinder and Katya Aster stood on opposite sides of their little defensive circle, but their movements were mirrored as they wove some kind of spell.

He wondered for a moment why Ray wasn't standing with them, adding his own formidable magic to the defences clustered around Yarra. But the question answered itself a moment later. Ray was crouched with Izrabella Dijon, letting the small white-haired girl lean on him as she poured her potent healing magic into Yarra's broken and bleeding form.

The other Mossmans were likewise occupied. Kelly and Matt were trying to revive Erryk, leaving Annika alone to add her strength to their defence. But even alone, the earth magic a single Mossman commanded was formidable. Annika's power alone was enough to make the foundations of the Cerulean Gardens shake.

Ray raised his head briefly, emerald eyes instantly locked with Royce's. There was no hate in Ray's gaze, no animosity, only desperation and a slight hint of impatient annoyance.

Ray didn't hate him for stealing away House Green. Ray didn't hate him for revealing the pledge to those who would use it to destroy them. Ray only cared for Yarra and his family, only cared about seeing them all live through this. The question of his lost lordship could be answered later. First, Royce had to make sure his errors didn't see them all dead.

'My magic grants me speed,' he said tightly. 'It grants me heightened awareness and agility. But at its base, at its most fundamental, my magic is but a fraction of what Charlotte can do. A fraction of her power.'

'I fail to see the significance of this,' Alexander said.

Royce wanted to shout at him. Alexander Sheresta had ruled House Orange for decades. How could he be this stupid, this slow? He was famed throughout the Rainbow and Verstra alike for his strategic mind, his unbeatable strategies and firm grasp of battlefield tactics. If he had lost that edge, then maybe Charlotte was right. Maybe they deserved to let this war destroy them.

'Oh' was all Alexander Sheresta said, his voice very small, face deathly pale.

'What is it?' Kayneth demanded. 'What?'

'Royce's magic is based on the manipulation of air,' Joseph Moon answered in an equally small voice. 'If Charlotte's magic were to fade as a result of this girl's death, then Royce's magic too would fade.'

'All magic at its most basic form can be represented by a house of the Rainbow,' Alexander Sheresta said, sheathing his weapon and stepping down. 'If they were all to lose their power, then magic itself would cease to exist.' He looked like he was swallowing a planet, but Alexander Sheresta spat out the final words. 'She cannot be allowed to die.'

Joseph Moon looked haunted, but it was clear he understood. 'It would be like killing magic itself.'

All eyes turned to and rested on Yarra, on where Izrabella Dijon worked diligently to heal all those ghastly life-threatening wounds. Even the shadows seemed to press closer, as if they too were aware of what was at stake.

Royce gazed at her with as much love and tenderness as he could, willing her to live not out of any personal attachment – for indeed, he still hated her and wished her locked away from the world – but because of what she now represented to them all: hope.

'She has to live,' he whispered.

33

Unearthing

Everyone resumed their seats, and although the very air was strained, a semblance of calm order returned to the convergence.

'Will she live?' Kayneth Kor asked.

Charlotte Goldenrod had remained standing, and although she had moved back to her place at the table, it was clear she had erected a shield of hard air around Yarra and Izrabella.

The latter raised her head. Sweat beaded her brow; pearls of it slipped through her silvery strands of hair. Her flame-red eyes burned as hot as Ferric's fire, but they were dulled by exhaustion.

'I have done all I can,' she said in a small voice.

'What does that mean?' Alexander Sheresta demanded.

Ray rubbed at his temples. The former lord of House Green stood with his family behind Charlotte. There had been a brief moment when Royce had thought Ray would challenge him for leadership then and there, but the two had merely locked eyes before Ray had taken his family over to House Yellow, to be welcomed by the Goldenrod cousins.

'Erryk was taken by vampires,' Ray said slowly, like he was too tired to pretend not to be annoyed by this whole situation. 'When we found her, she had already been bitten.'

'So have the Dijon girl heal her,' Kayneth spat.

Ray just shook his head. 'You don't understand. Whenever Yarra gets bitten by a vampire . . .,' Ray trailed off, crushed, defeated.

'She bites back,' Kelly finished. 'If a vampire bites her, Yarra bites back.'

And therein lay the problem.

177

Izrabella Dijon, however powerful her healing magic might be, could not halt the process of becoming a vampire. Vampire toxin reacted badly with magic, and Yarra was magic. That alone would have been hard for the small girl to heal. But if Yarra had bitten back . . . He could only hope the natural resistance she had to poisons and toxins would save her.

'So there's nothing we can do?' Ferric Oxblood asked.

Izrabella shook her small head, tears brimming from her eyes. Charlotte opened her arms and smothered the small girl within them.

'So that's it then. We're doomed.' Kayneth Kor spun in his seat, facing everyone one at a time. His eyes rested longest on Alexander. But the leader of House Orange had nothing to add.

Royce felt it the moment they all gave up – the crushing sadness and sorrow that blanketed them all, smothered them in darkness, darker than the writhing shadows, shadows that seemed to be waiting, watching.

A wheezing breath. A hacking cough.

'What is this? The Rainbow defeated? Really? Have a little more faith in me, would you? This is just insulting.'

Yarra shook as she forced herself first to sit and then to stand, and although Izrabella had healed her wounds, she was still coated in enough blood that Royce feared she'd topple over in an instant. But she glared at them, her slate-grey eyes cold from behind her matted tangle of night-black hair.

'I'm not dead yet.'

Ray heaved a long sigh. 'No, Yarra, but you soon will be.'

'This is hardly the first time I've been bitten by a vampire.'

'No, Yarra, but it is the first time you've been so close to death.'

The way Ray kept repeating her name . . . it was like he was trying to ground her, to remind her of who she was, keep her attention focussed solely on him.

'This is hardly the first time I've bitten them back either.'

'No, Yarra,' Ray repeated, 'but it is the first time you've been so close to death.'

'Is that why everyone is so defeated? Because the light almost went out? Because against the darkness, one small flickering flame was almost lost? The real fight hasn't even begun yet, and the colours collapse. You do remember that Jibrayne has raised an army, right? That there will be war?'

'We remember, Yarra, but there won't be anything left to fight for if you die.'

Yarra frowned, sucked on her lip, cleaning dried blood off a portion of it.

'Who is Jibrayne?' Kayneth Kor asked.

'Vampire we used to know,' Ray said distractedly, eyes glued to Yarra.

Royce could see the gears turning behind his emerald eyes, could see him size up Yarra's weakness, the strength Izrabella had managed to restore and the reserves that lay depleted.

'Will you heal, Erryk?' Ray asked her.

Yarra tilted her head to the side, quizzical. 'Can't Izrabella do it?'

'She could,' Ray said evenly, 'but I want you to.'

Because to heal others, Yarra must also heal herself. But the girl shook her head.

'He is fine. Lola and Lorelai did not harm him.'

'Can you be sure of that?'

Yarra nodded, and something shifted in Ray's expression, lingering concern over his brother lessening into relief.

'Hold up,' Alexander Sheresta called, raising a hand as well as his voice for silence. 'Who is this Jibrayne person? Who are Lola and Lorelai?'

'Lola and Lorelai are the vampires who kidnapped Erryk,' Ray said testily, 'and I already told you, Jibrayne was a vampire we used to know. A vampire who has raised an army and is probably the single driving factor behind this war.'

Now it was Kayneth who raised his voice. 'Back up! Let me get this straight. You used to know the vampire responsible for this war? *And you let them live?*'

Ray nodded.

'How do you even know this Jibrayne is even behind the war?' Alexander asked.

It was Alexander's own captain of the guard who answered. 'we have heard rumours of a vampire uprising,' he said, 'of werewolves and vampires working together. Is such a feat something Jibrayne could accomplish?'

Ray nodded again.

'Do you know where they are,' Kayneth asked, 'where they've based their armies?'

Shaking heads from across the room.

'We can find out,' Yarra croaked, straightening slightly. 'There is a way.'

Ray's face was so filled with desperation and sadness, Royce almost felt bad for asking him to force Yarra to use her powers as a seer. If it hurt him this much to see her offer herself up like this, how much must it hurt him to ask it of her? But he couldn't think about that now. He was leader of House Green, and he had a world to save.

'No . . .,' Charlotte Goldenrod said in a broken whisper. 'Yarra, no. You can't.'

Yarra turned exhausted and pain-filled grey eyes to the lord of House Yellow. Her mouth opened in what could have been a small, sad smile.

'I think that's the first time you've ever called me by my name,' Yarra said sadly, genuine tears in her eyes, 'but there is no other way.'

'There has to be!' Ferric Oxblood barked, small sparks bursting into being around his head. 'We cannot allow you to do this.'

Yarra paused. A strange expression crossed her face. It was smug triumph mixed with thoughtfulness and curiosity hidden under a mask of weariness that he knew was not faked, not entirely.

Royce was left with the distinct feeling she had planned this. That was the feeling her expression gave him. The rumble of delighted laughter from the shadows seemed to confirm as much – laughter that, this time, did not go unnoticed by the wider convergence.

Lords and leaders cast suspicious eyes into the gloom, seeking out eavesdroppers that would dare intrude on the Rainbow's secret meeting. Peering eyes found nothing. Only the taut paleness of Ray's face and the collective shuddering of the other Mossmans gave Royce any clue as to what the shadows hid – or who.

'I suppose . . .,' Yarra said, drawing out the word, 'that we could always ask the spies. The spies always know what's going on.'

'Spies?' Alexander Sheresta asked. 'You mean the Amaryllis family? They're all dead. Dies out years and years ago. You've gone mad, girl.'

Yarra smiled sweetly – or as sweetly as she could while covered head to foot in her own blood. It was a smile that plainly stated that her madness was not a new occurrence. The same smile was mirrored on Ray's face and the faces of Charlotte Goldenrod and Ferric Oxblood.

Yarra placed a hand to her head, like she had a headache or was trying to keep her brains from spilling out. 'I may be mad,' she said, 'but I am not wrong. The spies are alive and well.'

Kayneth Kor shook his head. 'Ridiculous.'

'What do you know of my family?' Yarra asked sweetly.

'Not much,' Kayneth admitted.

'And what do you know of the family whose house you now rule?'

'I know they were hunted, that they were spies, the best of the best.'

Yarra's smile was nothing short of lethal. 'And how was it that they were able to be hunted so effectively? If they were such good spies, surely, they knew how to disappear.'

Silence in the council halls.

'House Orange has red eyes, House Yellow has golden eyes, House Red has a temper as hot as their fire, and House Violet, well, House Violet has red hair.'

Kayneth's cherry-gold locks were suddenly very obvious, as were his children's red-brown, rust-coloured hair – a very clear deviant of red.

Yarra snorted. 'What? Did you think the world's best spies simply allowed themselves to be hunted and killed? Why, there are probably more Amaryllis branch members than all the other families put together.'

Dean and Lynda Couvrette turned accusatory eyes towards the Kor family. Kayneth stood ramrod straight, pale under his cherry-gold hair, his family still as stone behind him. All looked like they wanted nothing more than to disappear. Alexander and Theresa Sheresta looked down their noses at the family they had allied with for so long.

'But we have none of their powers,' Kayneth Kor said in a small voice, his face very pale. 'It's impossible.'

'It's very possible,' Yarra said, her head still in her hands. 'The spies are everywhere. And they no doubt know where Jibrayne has hidden her armies.'

'Well?' Dean Couvrette demanded. 'Do you know?'

Kayneth Kor shook his head, cherry-gold locks flying around his shoulders wildly.

Yarra shrugged dismissively. 'If he doesn't know, why not ask Joseph if he does?' She looked almost bored – disappointed, even – at the lack of collective brain cells being used to solve the simplest of puzzles. 'Moon is not an uncommon name,' she mused, picking at a nail, completely at ease. 'Moon is a name associated with darkness, with the night.' Yarra looked up and glared at them all with such exasperated annoyance, you could hear her eyes roll in her voice. 'And who do we know who has affiliations with shadows and the darkness of the night?' She fixed them all with her best schoolteacher look.

'The Amaryllis family,' Joseph Moon said at last, his voice scarcely more than a whisper as the darkness rumbled with laughter.

Clap. Clap. Clap.

Yarra raised her hands above her head and spun in a slow circle. And although not one member of the Rainbow moved even an inch, not a single lord or leader in the convergence moved a muscle, the clapping continued.

All the blood had drained from Ray's face to pool at his feet. He was ghostly pale, almost ashen. He fixed Yarra with terrified emerald eyes. 'You didn't . . .,' he hissed towards her.

Yarra ignored him.

Annika Mossman placed her hands on the hilts of her twin rapiers, her eyes darting through the shadows. Kelly and Matt positioned themselves closer together, putting themselves between Erryk and the darkness.

Royce was not the only one to notice the Mossmans' strange behaviour. Charlotte Goldenrod and Ferric Oxblood were watching the family strangely; all the surviving members of the original families were watching the Mossmans with open curiosity, curiosity that quickly became fear. Tangible fear was not something the other leaders could ignore. Soon, the whole convergence was blanketed in uneasiness.

'You didn't . . .,' Ray hissed again. 'Yarra, you couldn't have.'

'The little she-devil can do what she wants,' the shadows said, laughter rippling off every word.

In the silence that followed, Royce breathed just one word. 'Nifilious.'

'Who is Nifilious?' Dean Couvrette asked softly, as if speaking too loud would dispel the sense of security the silence had brought.

'An ancient god bound to the Rainbow,' Ferric replied with equal silence, 'the last line of defence for the knowledge House Green guards.'

'I thought that was a myth . . .,' Meredith Beryl breathed.

Charlotte Goldenrod turned to Ray, accusation in her eyes. 'Why is he here? What about the books?'

Ray flinched back, guilt rising to wipe the terror from his features.

'The books are fine,' Yarra said. She waved a hand sluggishly, rubbed her temples. 'Jibrayne would not dare go after them.'

'How can you be so sure?' Alexander Sheresta asked.

Nifilious chuckled, his shadowed hands running fingers down the spines of everyone who heard it. 'The little she-devil knows because the she-devil knows all.'

'That doesn't make sense,' Annika said, a quaver to her voice.

'Jibrayne hides her army in the Dead Lands,' Yarra said, 'She uses thousands of captured ghosts to hide them, uses the ghosts' magic keep them from our sight. She is poised to strike three lands at once, to push through Green and Yellow and Blue and move onto the rest of Verstra in one fell swoop.'

'Yarra,' Ray warned, 'stop. Riddles and rhymes are safer than this. You don't have to do this.'

But Yarra just smiled.

It was not until Ray said it that Royce realised it was true, that Yarra, ever the lover of cryptic clues and ridiculous rhymes, had spoken in clear, prefect, and precise sentences, that the longer she talked, the firmer she pressed her hands to her head, the tighter she gripped fistfuls of hair, the more she listed slightly to the side. This was the toll her magic took. This was what he had wanted to use to win this war.

'It is my magic,' she said firmly, gritting her teeth. 'Mine. And I will use it as I will.'

She raised stone-cold eyes to gaze at the convergence, her magic transforming the uncaring grey into tiny burning stars. Such power raging behind those eyes, such might, such rage and hatred and strength – a light against the dark.

A monster to fight the monsters.

'The Rainbow is united at last,' she said, 'and I'll be damned if I let this world fall to ruin.'

About the Author

Naomi is a nineteen-year-old author/student from Sydney, Australia. She has been writing since her early teen years. Escaping into worlds of her own creation from a very young age, reading books far beyond her years and writing what she loves. Throughout her school life Naomi's teachers were impressed with her creative writing ability and supportive of the fictional worlds she wrote about, providing valuable guidance as her writing began to grow. Now at only nineteen years of age, Naomi has graduated High School and began her university studies majoring in Climate Science and Anthropology. Between her part-time work and studies Naomi enjoys constructing her intricate fantasy worlds, painting, sculpting and any other artistic outlet she sets her mind to. Her limitless imagination fuelling her ever growing creative desires. Naomi lives in Sydney, Australia with her three younger brothers, parents and much loved family dog.

www.ingramcontent.com/pod-product-compliance
Lightning Source LLC
Chambersburg PA
CBHW020330110726
47898CB00003B/819